THE
JET RACER

ANDY DAVIDS

BLUE FORGE PRESS
Port Orchard, Washington

For information about film, reprint or other subsidiary rights, contact: blueforgegroup@gmail.com

Blue Forge Press is the print division of the volunteer-run, federal 501(c)3 nonprofit company, Blue Forge Group, founded in 1989 and dedicated to bringing light to the shadows and voice to the silence. We strive to empower storytellers across all walks of life with our four divisions: Blue Forge Press, Blue Forge Films, Blue Forge Gaming, and Blue Forge Records. Find out more at www.BlueForgeGroup.org

Blue Forge Press
7419 Ebbert Drive Southeast
Port Orchard, Washington 98367
blueforgepress@gmail.com
360-550-2071 ph.txt

CONTENT WARNING

This book contains subjects that may be triggering to some readers: Alcohol, bullying, child abuse, death (animal and character), emesis, fire, foster care, guns (reference), homophobia, hospitalization, misgendering, needles, pregnancy, profanity, PTSD, racism, religion, sex, sexism, stalking, suicide, transphobia, and violence.

Acknowledgments

The author would like to thank the following individuals for their expertise and knowledge in ensuring the accuracy of technical details in the story:

Joe Melatini

John Smithman

Karlene Petitt

JR Russell

Patrick Paris

Frank Baker

Chris Long

THE
JET RACER

ANDY DAVIDS

CHAPTER 1

It was a typical usual morning at Central City Jet Racing League Airfield. I sat at my desk in my room, waiting for Mike to arrive with breakfast. Having breakfast delivered was one of my favourite privileges as a professional jet racer. *Will it be French toast again, like the last three days?* I wondered. *Or something different?* There was a knock at the door.

"Good morning," Mike said in his Texan accent. He looked scruffy like he hadn't shaved for a few days. I wondered if he was trying to grow his beard out. He smiled as he handed me my plate. It was French toast indeed, for the fourth day in a row.

"Thanks," I said. "How are you doing?"

"My back's not acting up, so it's one of those better days."

I guess I really shouldn't have asked.

"Busy day today?" I asked.

"Have to finish delivering breakfast, and then I have to do the daily plane inspections."

"Sounds like you got your hands full."

"Before I forget, logs, please?"

I tore out the previous day's pages from my logbook and handed them to him. The National Jet Racing Association paid us for time spent on practice flights between races, and filling out the log sheets was like filling out time cards. Mike went back to pushing the food cart down the hallway. I looked out the window; it was a fantastic day for flying, with not a cloud to be seen. I checked the day's weather conditions and visibility report on my computer. Then I left my room after breakfast and went to the hangar.

"Morning, Vinnie, a great day to fly, isn't it?" I said to one of the other jet racers as I passed him in the hallway.

"I'd love to join you, but I have to get my physical today," Vinnie replied.

"You look tired. Did you sleep okay?" I asked.

"Nope, too much noise," he yawned. "Max again."

I giggled under my breath.

"Yep, another one of his little moments," Vinnie said. "Kept me up all night. Irene couldn't sleep either."

That made sense, as Irene's room was on the right of Max's, and Vinnie's was on the left.

"Looks like she's still sleeping," I said. "Her door's closed."

"You're probably right. Anyways, I got to get going. Have a good flight."

I was lucky to have the last room at the end of the hall, with nobody to my right. Julianne, next door on the left, just stayed up watching movies most nights, although I was so glad the day she finally got some headphones.

When I arrived at the hangar entrance, I tapped my key card on the door and placed my hand on the scanner. The automated security door slid open. Mike sat on a stool, touching up the paint on Vinnie's plane, filling in the scratches. We jet racers always wanted our planes to look presentable, even when we weren't racing.

"Just finished cleaning all the mud off your plane, so she's ready to fly," he said. He went back to painting. "Have a good flight."

"Thanks."

Max entered the hangar. "You ready to fly?" he asked.

He looked a bit lost in his thoughts.

"Everything okay?" I said to him.

"I had a dream that Juli was in my bed, and, damn, does she know ever how to show a guy a good time!" Max gave an obnoxious laugh. "I mean, look at that body. I swear, even if I were a woman, I'd still want her."

I rolled my eyes and glanced over at Mike. He winked at me and continued painting.

Max thought for a second. "Hell, that'd make me a lesbian. I've been with more girls than you your whole life, and I'd still choose her."

To be fair, she was good-looking.

We walked over to our lockers and grabbed our flight jackets.

"Would you mind helping me work on my barrel roll again? I'm still having some trouble with it," Max asked.

"Didn't I just go over it with you last week?" I sighed. *If only he'd stop forgetting every time I show him.*

"Had to do daddy-and-daughter stuff with Izzy yesterday."

That meant it was his visitation day with Izzy. *But what does that have to do with barrel rolls?*

"Are you saying you've forgotten what I've said?"

"My mind's a bit preoccupied," he replied.

I mean, Max could play the bass. Surely he wouldn't forget how after not playing for a while. Some might say it's like riding a bike, though I never learned how to ride a bike, so I couldn't strictly relate to that analogy. But I couldn't imagine a barrel roll being more complicated than playing bass. I couldn't play an instrument to save my life.

"That's understandable," I said.

"Trust me; it's not easy being a dad and not getting to see your daughter much because you're too busy practising for races. She's always in the back of my mind."

"Before we fly, I need to show you something," I said to him, thinking that some visuals might make it easier for him to remember. I sat down at the table next to the lockers. Max sat beside me, shifting his chair slightly so his knees weren't hitting the bottom of the table. I took my pen and notebook out of the pocket of my flight jacket and tore a blank page out of the notebook.

"You know what this is, right?" I said as I drew a simple diagram on the page.

"Yes, a barrel roll."

I drew a diagram of a barrel roll with five small triangles representing the plane's orientation.

"It helps to think of the motion like you're running your wheels along the inside of a barrel. Got it?"

Max nodded.

"Now, what's happening here?" I asked as I pointed to the first triangle in the diagram.

"The nose is being pulled up."

"Yes. I try to aim for forty-five degrees from the horizon."

I drew a diagram of a line to represent the horizon, with another line pointing approximately forty-five degrees up from it beside the barrel roll diagram.

"And then what's next?" I pointed to the second triangle.

"Push right to start the roll?" he said. There was some uncertainty in his voice. "Then push left to finish the roll?"

"Yes, and you want to make the entire roll smooth and graceful. Ready to try it?"

He nodded.

"You should keep this for reference," I said, handing him the diagram.

He stuffed it into his pants pocket, and we went to our planes. Mike always did a good job touching up those scratches and cleaning the dirt off the wheels. Max and I did our pre-flight checks. I climbed into the cockpit of my plane, #80, and shut the canopy. I switched the avionics on and said a quick "Jet Racer Eight Zero, avionics on" into my headset.

Max responded. "Copy. Jet Racer Six Seven, avionics on."

I taxied out of the hangar, with Max forming up to my

right as we made our way down to the end of the runway. The single runway at the airfield was wide enough for precisely two planes to take off together.

"Jet Racers Eight Zero and Six Seven requesting takeoff from runway two three," I said into the radio.

"Jet Racers Eight Zero and Six Seven, line up and wait," the air traffic controller announced. "Jet Racers Eight Zero and Six Seven, you are cleared for takeoff from runway two three."

The rumble of the powerful engine droned dully through my headset. I felt an intense rush of excitement as the G-forces pushed me back against the seat. The trees and the airfield building became smaller as I took off from the runway.

"Jet Racers Eight Zero and Six Seven, monitor this frequency and switch to one zero one point two," the air traffic controller said.

"Copy that." We switched our radios to channel 101.2. It was the channel for pilots to talk casually on.

"I'll do a barrel roll first, and then it's your turn," I said through the radio.

I levelled myself with the horizon before rotating the plane on its lateral axis. I felt the force of gravity lift me out of my seat as the sky and ground switched places for a second before I completed the roll. I then watched as Max made the slight dip down. I waited for him to roll, but he seemed hesitant.

"What're you waiting for?" I asked.

"Nothing," Max replied.

"Make sure you lose a few knots before you go for it."

"Alright." But he didn't seem to be slowing down even after I had told him.

"You'll be fine," I reassured him.

"I'm nervous." I could hear Max's voice tremble.

"You've done it before."

I watched him level himself with the horizon and pull up ever so slightly as though he was about to begin the manoeuvre, only to climb back up and make a sharp turn left instead.

"Everything okay?" I asked, wondering why he hadn't completed the manoeuvre.

"I'm fine," he replied, but his voice stuttered slightly.

"Remember, lose a few knots."

"Alright, alright." He was beginning to sound frantic. He pulled the nose up, went in for the roll, and quickly followed it up with a second roll.

"Two in a row!" Max bragged. "Here goes another one!"

He sure seems hyped up now.

"You're going too fast," I said.

He slowed down a tad and went in for the roll, executing it successfully before turning around and pulling two more in a row.

"Someone's sure having fun."

"Here goes some more!" Max said. The excitement in his voice was growing.

I watched him set himself up for the manoeuvre, but I could see him going too fast again.

"Remember what I said before you roll?" I reminded him.

But he still didn't slow down. I felt things would not turn out how he wanted, but I didn't want to waste time arguing with him.

"Max!" I shouted into the headset.

He did not respond, nor did he slow down.

I looked at him out the side of my cockpit. His plane had spun upside down.

"Let go of the stick right now!" I shouted. I could feel the sweat dripping down my forehead.

"I almost got it!"

Now it seemed like I was more nervous than him. Perhaps the excitement made him forget how scared he'd been at first.

"Let go; you'll right yourself."

"I got this," Max reassured himself. "I got this."

"Let go of the stick, now!" I shouted on the radio. My heart was pounding.

"I got it," Max repeated to himself. "I got it."

I sighed with relief as his plane flipped back to right-side up. Max levelled himself back with the horizon again.

Knowing how close the top of his head was to the canopy, I could only imagine how nervous he must have been when he spun himself upside down. At least I never had to worry about feeling like I would hit my head on the canopy when doing inverting manoeuvres, being shorter than him.

"I need more practice," Max said.

"Do you want to try a few more?"

"I think I'm okay for now," he replied. Given his stress, he probably needed a break from barrel rolls.

"I think I'm hungry now. What about you?"

"Yeah, me too," I replied. I looked at the clock on my flight instruments. It was 12:05 p.m. "Meet you at the lunchroom." I switched my radio back to the airfield's channel.

"Jet Racer Eight Zero requesting landing on runway two three."

"Jet Racer Six Seven requesting landing on runway two three," Max said into the radio.

"Jet Racers Eight Zero and Six Seven, you are cleared to land on runway two three."

Back at the hangar, we stowed our planes and returned our flight jackets to our lockers. Mike had just finished painting Vinnie's plane. He was standing at the sink washing the paintbrushes.

"It's hard to believe how much I'm sweating," Max said, wiping his forehead with his sleeve. "Especially since it's so cold up there."

"Me too," I replied. "Shall we eat?"

"Sure," Max replied. "You coming, Mike?"

"I'll join you once I'm done with these brushes."

Max tapped his key card on the reader. I followed him out of the hangar and headed toward the lunchroom. The smell of food made my stomach grumble even before entering the lunchroom. *Smells like some kind of pasta*, I thought. Irene and Vinnie were already sitting at the table when we arrived.

I lined up at the food counter. Macaroni and cheese, spaghetti with tomato sauce, garden salad with ranch dressing, and roast beef sandwiches were on the menu for the day. I went for the roast beef while Max had the macaroni.

"How was your flight, Jay?" Irene looked up from her plate as Max and I sat at the table. I could tell she was trying to avoid eye contact with Max. *Perhaps she doesn't want to be mad at him for keeping her up all night,* I thought.

"Not bad," I said.

"At least I didn't lose my plane," Max added, grumbling.

"That's a good sign," Vinnie said. He took a sip of water from his glass.

"Yeah, don't want to lose your plane again," Irene teased. "That's for sure."

"What happened?" I cut in.

"Do you really need to know?" Max sighed.

"Just wondering," I took a bite of my sandwich.

"It was supposed to be a great day to fly, but some dark storm clouds rolled in. I decided to start heading back to the hangar, but then my engine started acting up," Max explained. He was starting to stutter again.

"That's not good," I said.

"Soon after, my engine failed. So I was left with one option." He paused and cleared his throat. I could see that he was shaking a bit. "Ditch her in the lake and swim to shore."

"Couldn't you land on the beach?" I asked.

"It was too rocky, so I made a forced water landing into the lake because my engine was deadstick," Max explained, slamming his hand on the table to describe the landing. "Little did I know that I was headed for shallow water. I got a few bruises trying to brace myself on landing."

"Well, at least you weren't hurt," Irene said. Even though she was talking to Max, she still avoided eye contact.

"Your plane must've gotten some nasty dents, though," I said.

"The biggest dent was to my paycheque," Max replied. "But waiting on the beach with wet pants and boots wasn't exactly pleasant."

"I bet," Irene replied. "I get pretty cranky when my shoes get soaked in the rain."

"Believe me, it was awful," Max said.

"Maybe you should have been more careful," Irene said.

"Do you think an engine problem was my fault?" Max said to Irene before turning to me. "Mike wasn't too happy about it, as you could probably guess."

"Did he scream at you?" I asked.

"Not exactly. He just bitched and moaned about how much work he had cut out for him, all those extensive repairs and whatnot."

Julianne walked up to the table, balancing her plate on her laptop.

"Saved a spot for you," Max said, pointing to the empty spot on the bench beside him. Julianne sat down and put her laptop on the table beside her plate.

I turned to Vinnie and pointed to the salad and assortment of steamed vegetables next to a small serving of spaghetti on his plate. "Eating healthy?"

"Yeah," he replied. "Not feeling a hundred percent lately."

"Coming down with a cold?" Irene asked, taking a sip of orange juice.

"Haven't been sleeping well," Vinnie replied. "Something's been on my mind."

"Girls?" Max cut in, turning his head toward Vinnie.

"Nah." He paused to take a bite of salad. "Just worried about the nationals."

"Hey, you should be proud of yourself," I replied. "You and Juli are the only rookies in the nationals this year."

"For sure," Vinnie said. "It's pretty awesome that everyone in our league made it to the nationals."

"Yeah, definitely." I nodded.

"By the way, this is delicious spaghetti," Vinnie said, finishing the last of the spaghetti on his plate. "Reminds me of my mom's cooking."

If an Italian person was comparing that spaghetti to home cooking, it must have been something. I couldn't remember any of my Italian classmates saying that about the school cafeteria pasta years ago.

"Sounds like they know what they're doing," I replied. "Should try it next time."

"Speaking of the nationals," Max said. "I don't have a good feeling about Andrew Mayer joining us."

"How come?" I asked. I had heard Andrew's name before, but I did not know much about him or what could be so bad about him. All I knew was that he was moving from the

New England Jet Racing League to our league.

"Raced with him in the nationals two years ago, thinks he's God's gift to the NJRA just because he's a second-generation jet racer. He's a typical Masshole as well, accent and everything." Max said. He wasn't exactly fond of people from Massachusetts.

"Textbook example of a spoiled kid," Irene added. "When he's got nothing to complain about, he's bound to find something."

"But Ash's a second generation, too," I said. "And he doesn't get all whiny."

"Ash is Ash, and Andrew is Andrew," Irene replied. "Don't go comparing apples to oranges."

"Would you guys mind keeping it down?" Julianne looked up from the screen and took a bite of macaroni. "I'm watching something."

"She's so cute when she's mad," Max whispered to me, smirking.

Mike walked into the lunchroom. He had changed his clothes, though he still had a few drips of paint in his greying hair. "Mind if I join ya'll?" he asked. He sat next to me and put his cane against the side of the bench.

"Not at all," I replied. "How did the painting go?"

"Slow and steady. Need to rest my achy back now," Mike said, rubbing the right side of his back. "Hope ya'll never have to eject."

I had heard enough from Mike about the consequences of ejecting from a plane to hope that it didn't happen to me, but at the same time, dying in a fiery crash was indeed the worse of two evils.

"I hope so, too," Vinnie replied.

"At least you still work for the NJRA," I said. I'd felt sorry for the poor guy ever since I'd found out how much pain he lived with. It wasn't hard to see why that poor guy always complained about his back. I could only imagine how frustrating it must be for him to watch us fly all the time when he couldn't anymore. It made me appreciate even more all the hard work he put into maintaining our planes and the airfield.

"Could be doing more if I'd gone back to school," Mike said. "You ever think about going back, Jay?"

"Nope," I replied. "What's the point?"

"Something good to have in your back pocket," Mike replied.

"I didn't feel like I was getting anywhere either," Irene said. "Even after two years of university."

"What did you study?" Vinnie asked.

"Went into computer science thinking it'd be interesting, then got bored and switched to a general major. Didn't finish that either. Just decided university wasn't for me."

"Oh, I wouldn't be stuck bringing breakfast and mail every day if I'd gone back." Mike paused and took a couple of bites of spaghetti. "Speaking of mail, I forgot to give this to you earlier."

He handed me an envelope. Not even bothering to look at the return address, I ripped it open and pulled out the folded letter.

Dear Jayson David Smith,

I know it's been a while since you've heard from me. But don't worry; you're not in trouble or anything. I've told the guys at your airfield's office that I will be visiting you in a day or two, depending on my schedule. I hope life is treating you well. I will be cheering for you at the nationals.

Talk to you soon.

Shauna Ritchie
Youth Social Worker
Central City Senior High

"Who's the lucky one?" Max said, then made kissing sounds with his lips.

"Nobody." I sounded like a secretive teenager hiding something from his parents but didn't know what else to say.

"Oh, really?" Max replied playfully. He tried to grab the letter out of my hand.

"People still write letters?" Vinnie cut in.

"Wish someone still did that for me," Max said. "Back when I went on tour for weeks with my band, I'd write a letter home to my wife, who was then my girlfriend, every chance I got."

"But texting is a lot faster," I said.

"I wrote them on bar napkins or hotel notepads, whatever was around," Max explained. "She saved every one of them. Sure, texting is faster, but she always said how much she loved seeing my handwriting."

"That's very thoughtful of you," I replied.

"So what you got there, Jay?" Max asked.

"Just a letter from a teacher from my old school."

I didn't know how to explain that she was a school social worker without sounding too much like I was some troubled kid with behaviour problems, though, in all honesty, that was who I was. It had been many years since I'd heard anything from Ms. Ritchie. The letter brought back all sorts of memories, from the first time a school security guard sent me to her office when he found me bruised and bleeding after a fight at lunchtime to the last time I saw her when she practically begged me to stay in school.

"But you haven't been in school for a while," Max added.

"She wanted to get in touch with me again since she found out I'm in the nationals."

"Fair enough," Max replied.

"Will your daughter be at the nationals, by the way?" Vinnie asked Max.

"She doesn't come to races. Not since she was at my first race."

"Doesn't like the noise?" Vinnie asked.

"The smell of burning fuel bothers her," Max explained. He was stuttering again. I could see him shaking as he held back some tears. "Thanks to her mom burning the house down in the middle of the night years back."

"That woman's an ex for good reasons," Mike replied.

"No shit," Max sighed. "It's obvious I'm more concerned about Izzy than she could ever be."

"Of course," Mike said. "She's your daughter."

"Whenever I talk to Izzy, she says it feels like it was only yesterday. Especially because the puppy died," he explained in a shaky voice before taking a sip of water. "Izzy didn't see Fluffy die, but I had to grab her hand to stop her from running back inside to get him. She was bawling her eyes out, I tell you."

"Really sorry to hear that," I said.

"Oh, Fluffy was like her best friend," Max added.

I could almost see the glisten in Max's eyes as he mentioned the puppy, but he was able to keep a straight face.

CHAPTER 2

The next morning, I was returning to my dorm room from the showers. I could see the breakfast cart from the end of the hallway. Mike was early that day.

"Jay, here's your breakfast." Mike handed me my plate as I arrived at my room. On it were two soggy-looking pancakes next to a heap of scrambled eggs and some burnt bacon.

"Shauna Ritchie called a few minutes ago. She said she'd be here in about an hour."

That meant I had an hour to clean up my room so it wouldn't be messy when she arrived. I grabbed my logs and handed them to Mike.

Max opened his door and stood in the doorway. "Is there a letter from the association?" he asked.

"Let's see." Mike flipped through the mail tray on top of the breakfast cart. "Not yet."

"Something happen?" I asked.

"Just my waiver," he replied. "Have to renew it every year."

I would never understand what it was like to need a

waiver just to be allowed to fly since I didn't exceed the NJRA's height limit. I was a whole foot shorter than him. I had always been self-conscious about my height, in any case. I was always the shortest male student in the entire class.

In my first year of high school, I was still wearing kids' clothes. I dreaded back-to-school shopping, where I would spend hours flipping through racks of clothes with cartoon characters, monster trucks, and dinosaurs, searching for something I wouldn't be mortified to wear in public.

I sat down at my desk and ate my breakfast. The pancakes were undercooked, and the eggs were all runny. I didn't know why the kitchen couldn't cook anything well for breakfast except French toast. Perhaps day five of French toast would have been acceptable after all.

I rifled through my dresser, trying to decide what to wear. I wanted to leave a good impression on Ms. Ritchie. Ripped jeans and lumberjack shirts had been a thing of the past in favour of nicer clothes, such as V-neck t-shirts and khakis. I pulled on a navy-blue V-neck and took a pair of khakis off their hanger in the closet. They were slightly wrinkled, but they would do.

I picked up all my books off the floor and placed them on the dresser in a neat pile. I even made sure that the rug was perfectly centred between my bed and the couch. I took a moment to admire my work for a second. I rarely took the time to clean up.

I left the door open so Ms. Ritchie wouldn't have to knock. I sat on my bed and decided to read to help calm my nerves. I picked up last month's issue of *Modern Pilot* magazine from the top of the book pile.

I heard Mike's voice from down the hallway. I closed the magazine and put it back on the book pile. I stuck my head out the door and saw him at the end of the hallway; Ms. Ritchie was following behind him.

I stood at the doorway waiting for her. I could feel my palms and my face getting sweaty as memories of high school came back to me: every single time I was sent to her office, and of course, every single time I overheard my name when I saw her talking to another teacher in the hallway. As much as she probably thought I was a troubled student in high school, she was one of the few people who seemed to understand me – even when my adoptive parents, who raised and later adopted me, didn't. I was glad she had gotten in touch with me. There was something special about her making a point to visit me.

"Hi, Ms. Ritchie," I said. She sat on the couch while I sat on my bed across from her.

"You can just call me Shauna since we're not at school now."

"Then, hi, Shauna."

"It's been a while since I've seen you, Jayson," she said. "I like your clothes, by the way."

"I figured it was time I got new clothes. I mean, I'm twenty-one now; I figured it was time I grew up."

"They look great on you," she replied. "Nice and clean and comfortable."

Clean was the right word, especially compared to the mud-stained, ripped jeans she used to see me in. She pointed to the Ziggy Stardust poster on my closet door. "I see you're still a Bowie fan."

"Some things don't change."

"My brother got to see him in Oregon on his final tour. He said it was a great show. Jayson, how are you doing here?"

"Great. I love flying, and I'm excited about nationals coming up," I replied.

"Are you getting along with everyone?"

"For the most part. But there is this one guy who's been getting on my nerves lately," I replied.

"How so?"

"He just always talks about sex," I said. I paused for a second. "It makes me uncomfortable."

"Why does it make you uncomfortable?"

"I don't know. It always makes me uncomfortable when people talk about sex around me."

"I'm sure everyone has something that makes them feel that way," she answered. "Other than that, is everything okay?"

"It's just, uh," I stuttered, sniffling a bit. Seeing her face again brought so many memories back, as well as hearing her voice and seeing those black sheepskin boots she always used to wear.

"What is it?"

"Well, uh, it's like, a lot of old memories are coming back."

"I can see that something's bothering you. Do you mind sharing what those memories are?"

"I can't even think about anything related to high

school without feeling so ashamed of myself," I felt myself tearing up. I stood up and grabbed the box of tissues from my desk. I didn't know why it had taken me so long to realize I really should have given things some second thought before acting on them.

"That's a good sign. It means you've learned from your mistakes."

I nodded.

"But you can't forget to thank me for keeping you out of trouble when you and Craig got caught stealing from Walmart."

"You're right," I replied, sniffling. I could not have been more grateful to Ms. Ritchie, even though I didn't attend school anymore. I could barely remember Craig talked me into skipping math class that afternoon. I even went to Walmart and returned that t-shirt, though Craig proudly wore his.

"You've made your mistakes, but at least you're on the right track now. I mean, look, you're the youngest pilot in this year's Nationals."

I nodded again, blowing my nose.

"Just remember, you're a good person, like you've always been."

"I wouldn't call myself a model student."

"I can't think of many students I would call model students over the years," she said. "You've made mistakes. Now life goes on."

"I guess I just give in to pressure too easily." I wiped my tears. I must say, being in the NJRA taught me a lot about not giving in under pressure.

"You just needed some direction. That's true of a lot of young people these days."

"I remember signing up for the weight training club and quitting after the first week," I said. "Mr. Cole suggested I sign up to keep me busy after school."

"And, if I remember, you were fed up with how the guys treated the girls."

I nodded. Only two girls were in the club, and all the other guys would openly talk about them and make rude comments. And they were always eyeing the girls up and down, not to mention all the change room chat about who would 'make the first move' and when.

"They even went around telling people in the hallway that I was gay because I wasn't interested in staring at girls' bodies," I said.

"Are you going out with anyone now?" she asked. That question alone made me uncomfortable.

"I'm just not interested."

"Interested in a relationship? Or in women?"

"I'm not exactly interested in anyone that way. I can't remember liking girls much. Or boys, for that matter."

"Have you ever felt anyone else was attracted to you?" she asked.

She had never brought up this topic with me when I was in high school. Then again, I hadn't given it much thought back then, either.

"I could've sworn the other guys were checking me out in the shower during PE. It made me feel awkward." I paused to think of my next words as I tried to avoid eye contact with her. "It was, uh, like there was something dirty on my skin I couldn't wash off."

"Did you ever tell anyone how you felt?"

"I didn't think anyone would take me seriously. They'd tell me I had to find the right person, and then my hormones would kick in and do the rest. Deep down, I wish I didn't even have those hormones."

"I take you seriously, and your feelings are completely valid."

I reached for another tissue. There was a warm and comforting feeling inside me. It was the first time anyone told me those feelings were valid.

"Have you ever thought you might be asexual?" she asked.

My eyes widened. I hadn't heard that word since grade ten science, and then it was used to describe amoeba reproduction.

"I don't think so." I blew my nose again. "I mean, I've, uh, I've certainly felt, um, excited before."

"People who are asexual experience sexual arousal too."

"Really?" I said.

"Sexual arousal is the body's physical response. It doesn't necessarily mean you feel attracted to anyone," she explained.

"So I can be asexual and still feel turned on?"

"Yes. Being asexual is nothing to be ashamed of, and there's nothing wrong with feeling turned on either," she said.

"But at the same time, I have literally no interest in sex in any way, shape, or form," I said. Every time I tried to pretend to have any interest, it felt a bit odd, like something wasn't right. In the two years I'd been in the NJRA, I hadn't had a single affair or even hooked up with anyone within the association, even though that seemed to be the norm for many other racers.

"I don't even like the idea of falling in love," I added.

"Oh, tell me about it. I'm not asexual, and I'm not too fond of the idea either. I've already been through two divorces and a handful of relationships that never worked out."

"But why would anyone want to be asexual?" I asked, still confused.

"Nobody specifically wants to be asexual, just like nobody *wants* to be gay, bi, or straight. It's just another sexuality," she explained. "It's simply the way you are, just like the way relationships don't work for me."

"I've always known I don't fit in, for one reason or another."

"And I've always known that you are a bit different in your own way."

"It's the reason I like David Bowie a lot."

"He was an extravagant character who was not afraid to be who he was. I'm sure he sometimes felt like he didn't fit in too."

"Man, if only I could pull off some of those outfits," I said with a smile.

"Your new look is great," she replied. "So, the

nationals are coming up pretty fast. Are you excited?"

"I'm a bit nervous but feeling good at the same time."

"I'm sure you'll do great. My brother and I were watching the west coast qualifier on TV when I saw your name. I shouted, 'Oh my God, I know him!' I don't think I've ever seen you looking more confident than when the camera was on you after the race."

"I was still nervous. I guess I'm just good at hiding it on camera."

"Just remember that I will always be your fan no matter where you finish in any race. Winning is good, but more important is enjoying yourself. It's your first time in the nationals, and I know you'll do great."

"Thanks."

"I have a meeting at the school board, so I'd better get going. If you ever want to chat more, I'd be happy to visit again. Don't think of me as the school social worker anymore. Think of me as an old friend who only wants the best for you."

"I appreciate it."

"All the best next week," she said as she hugged me. As she left, she shut the door for me.

I stood up and walked over to my Ziggy Stardust poster. I thought about how great he looked with his striped outfit, platform boots, and long red hair. I scrolled through my David Bowie playlist on my computer and clicked on "Life on Mars." I was about to lay back and relax for a bit when I heard a knock on the door.

"Come in." I turned the volume down slightly. Mike walked in with another guy who looked a couple of years older than me. He was almost six feet tall with had dark brown hair.

"Jay, this is Andrew," Mike said. "Feel free to introduce yourself."

Mike turned around and walked away, leaving Andrew outside my room. Andrew scrunched his eyebrows as he looked at me, not saying a word. So this was Andrew Mayer, the bratty guy who had just switched over from New England Jet Racing League and had flown in the nationals before.

"Just got here?" I asked.

"Yup, just landed an hour ago," he replied.

"You must be tired."

"I'm fine; spent last night in Montana."

"Ah, at Big Sky Jet Racing League?"

"Just a small town airport. Wasn't even a couch to crash on," he answered.

"Didn't make it to Big Sky's airfield?"

"If you really want to know, I was nearly out of fuel and needed to land." He sounded annoyed.

"Slept in your plane?"

"It's no big deal," he said, rubbing the right side of his neck. "Aside from my neck being a little achy."

I guess I would take sleeping in my plane at a small airport over making a deadstick landing in the middle of nowhere.

"What brought you to Central City?" I asked.

"Too much drama back at New England; got sick of people over there."

"Sounds like a good reason to leave," I responded. Or

maybe he was the one being a total dick, and they were the ones that didn't want him around.

"Well, *you* look like you've had it with something," he said.

"Long story." It was like he'd read my mind or something. Or maybe I was looking a bit exhausted?

"I know you're nervous about the nationals," he said with an eye roll. I could tell he was trying to sound like a wisegeek as he said that.

"I guess so."

"Maybe you should go fly?" he suggested. "Help take your mind off things?"

"Maybe later."

"Well, I'm going," he replied. "Care to join?"

"But you've been flying for days straight," I said. "Don't you want to relax?"

"Didn't say I was going right now."

"Good, because I just want to relax for a bit."

Andrew left, shutting the door behind him. I turned the volume back up and sat down on my bed. "Rebel Rebel" was playing. I took *Advanced Jet Racing Strategies* off my desk, flipped it open, and began reading from where I had left off a few days before. I shut the book after just two pages. I picked up the *Modern Pilot* magazine from the pile on my dresser. I put it down again and decided to sit back and listen to David Bowie instead.

There was another knock at the door. *Not Andrew again,* I thought.

"Come in." I turned down my speakers.

It wasn't Andrew. It was Al, the airfield's office assistant.

"Don't mean to bother you," he said.

"No worries." I smiled.

"Rob from Central Radio called. He wanted to remind you about the interview at seven tonight. Here's the address for the studio." He handed me a piece of paper.

"Thanks." I had forgotten about the interview. I would have missed it if Al hadn't reminded me.

He left. I shut the door and turned the music back up. I flopped onto my bed and flipped open *Advanced Jet Racing Strategies*. I managed to read an entire chapter before my David Bowie playlist reached its end. Silence filled my room for a moment, only to be filled by the faint rumble of jet engines outside. It must have been Andrew flying with the others out there. I couldn't help wondering what the real reason for him leaving New England was and why, of all the leagues, he'd chosen Central City. *Maybe because Max is in it, he thinks it must be a good league or something.*

I clicked on a random album on the media player, which happened to be Tool's *Lateralus*. I returned to my bed and read another chapter of *Advanced Jet Racing Strategies* before putting the bookmark in it and placing it on the floor beside my bed. I got barely halfway through *Lateralus* when I decided to change the album again, deciding that I didn't quite feel like listening to it. I chose another Tool album, *10,000 Days*. I zoned out to the drummer's beat in the first song, "Vicarious." Max once told me that song was played in something called "five four," which had to do with the number of beats the drummer was playing.

I decided to go out to fly with Andrew and the others. After all, a bit of practice never hurt. I turned off the music and shut my computer down. I put on my pilot boots and made my way to the hangar. The automated door was open. Mike was standing in the doorway, spraying the track with WD-40.

"Have a good flight," he said, looking at me for a second. Then he went back to cleaning the door track.

I looked past the open hangar doors and up into the sky. I could see Vinnie's solid blue #37 and Julianne's yellow and orange #10. I'd never seen the purple and black plane #33, so that must've been Andrew's. There was another plane in the distance, too far away to make out its number or colour. As it flew closer, I could recognize the livery of Irene's #52 with the gold dragons against a red background.

I climbed into the cockpit of #80. I put my headset on and switched on the avionics.

"Jet Racer Eight Zero, requesting takeoff from runway two three," I said as I taxied out of the hangar and onto the runway.

"Jet Racer Eight Zero, you are clear for takeoff from runway two three," the air traffic controller responded.

I headed down the runway at full throttle. The trees in the mountains in the distance became a solid green carpet as I climbed higher and higher above terra firma.

"Tower to Jet Racer Eight Zero, monitor this frequency, switch to channel one zero one point two."

"Glad you could join us." I heard Vinnie's voice through

the headset. I watched him dive down into a vertical loop in front of me. *He's getting good at that.* Julianne followed suit and made a vertical loop herself. She had definitely improved since I'd helped her with that manoeuvre the first day she arrived.

"Not perfect, but getting there," she said.

"Nicely done," I replied.

"Heh, you call those vertical loops?" Andrew teased.

I watched as #33 flew a vertical loop. The smoke trailing behind formed an almost perfect circle. He climbed back up, levelled with the horizon, and weaved between me and Vinnie in a long, fluid stream of aileron rolls. He then went straight into an Immelmann loop in front of me.

"Flew my first airshow at seventeen," Andrew bragged.

"Now that's something," Julianne said, her voice shocked.

"Yeah, with my dad's Skybolt," Andrew said.

"I'm impressed," Vinnie replied.

"Friendly reminder," Andrew added sarcastically. "Gregory Mayer's my dad."

The name rang a bell, but it took me a few seconds to remember that Gregory Mayer was a two-time NJRA national champion forced to give up his racing career after a SCUBA diving accident on vacation in Hawaii. It made sense that Andrew had spent most of his life around planes.

Andrew did a climbing spin before levelling out and diving into a vertical loop, a white trail of smoke following behind him.

"You sure got moves," Julianne said through the radio.

"Why do you practise with smoke?" I asked. I never saw the point. With no crowd around, it's just a waste of smoke oil. I guess Andrew was that eager to show off.

"Of course I do. It helps show off my moves better," Andrew said. "Let's see yours, Jay."

Uhhhhh, okay then.

I turned my smoke system on to keep up with him. I flew a couple of circles around him, trying to decide what manoeuvre to do. There was no way I could get my vertical loop as perfectly round as his, or even Vinnie's, for that matter.

"Going to dance for us?" Andrew said on the radio. "Or are you more of a slow dancer?"

I started with two aileron rolls in a row and pulled upwards into an Immelmann turn. I attempted to replicate his upright climbing spin, only for it to turn out more like forty-five degrees. I shut off my smoke system.

"Shouldn't've dropped out of dance class, huh?" Andrew taunted. He laughed into the radio. I had a feeling it would take some time to get used to him.

CHAPTER 3

I took my tray and sat down at the table next to Irene.

"Guess Andrew's not coming for lunch," she said.

"He told me he wasn't," I replied.

"He looked okay when he got out of the plane," Julianne said. She put her headphones on and started watching a movie on her laptop.

"Something happen to him?" Max asked. He put his tray on the table and sat between Irene and Julianne. "I was on a call with my daughter."

"He made a pancake landing," Vinnie explained. "Scraped the underside of his plane pretty badly."

"That's what he gets for being so cocky," Irene said.

"Mike's making sure he's okay," I said. "Andrew's more upset about the damage to the plane than anything else."

"That's going to hurt his paycheque," Max added.

I passed Andrew's dorm room on the way back to mine after lunch. His door was open, and he was sitting on his bed, holding an ice pack against his left collarbone.

"What're you looking at, Jay?"

"Just wanted to make sure you're okay."

"Don't worry about me," he replied, sulking as he glared at me. "Worry about yourself."

I sighed as I turned around and continued walking, leaving his door open. *What a jerk.* Julianne's door was open. She was sitting at her desk with her laptop and staring at the screen, but she wasn't watching a movie.

She looked over at me from the screen. "Hi, Jay."

Her body language was nonchalant, but I could see the look on her face that something wasn't right.

"Is something wrong?"

Julianne turned her chair around to face me. "Might as well talk since you're here."

I shut the door and sat on the floor, even though the bed looked more comfortable. It felt odd to sit in a girl's room with the door shut, even though we were just chatting.

"Max's been acting a bit creepy," she said.

"What do you mean?" I knew he was attracted to her, but I never felt it was creepy.

"Last week, I wanted to go out and fly by myself, and he asked to join me even when I told him I wanted to fly alone," Julianne explained. "When I got back to the hangar, he stood in the doorway watching me take off my flight jacket, like literally eyeing me."

"Yikes, that does sound uncomfortable," I replied. "He should stick to hitting on girls his age."

"Yeah, I mean, for God's sake, he's thirty-seven, and I'm twenty-two. I mean, in training camp, there was this older guy who had a thing for girls strapped into safety harnesses."

"Did he creep on them?"

"Security caught him sleeping naked, strapped in the seat of a training simulator one night. The security footage showed he'd been playing with himself there earlier. He was kicked out and never heard from again."

"Hope they cleaned that seat well." I could not help but smirk at my comment.

"You can see why there're so few women in the NJRA."

I nodded.

"I'm treated like I'm a Barbie doll who flies." Julianne sighed, twirling her hair with her fingers. "It's unbelievable how many people can't take a girly girl seriously. And today, I overheard Max talking about a dream where he saw me naked. I wouldn't be surprised if Max flies with no pants on when I'm around, just thinking about me."

I let that image sink in for a second.

"Perhaps that's why they call it the cockpit," Julianne said, laughing.

I wasn't sure whether to laugh with her just to go along with the joke. I wanted to break away from that conversation as it was getting too awkward.

"Well, I have to go check my email now," I said.

"See you in a bit," she replied.

I returned to my room and shut the door. The image of that guy spending the night naked in a training simulator left an icky feeling on my skin. I picked up the month-old issue of *Modern Pilot* off the floor and tried to read some of it. A couple of pages into the magazine, I noticed a full-page picture of Max next to a headline that said, 'An Interview with

Max Erikson, the Man behind the Height.' I ripped out the pages of the interview and tossed them into the trash. But as I flipped through the rest of the magazine, I stumbled across another picture of him in an ad for the nationals. I tossed the entire magazine into the garbage can and placed it outside my door so Mike would throw it out in the morning.

Just as I closed the door again, someone knocked on the other side. I opened the door. It was Vinnie.

"I'm going bowling tonight," he said. "Want to join me?"

"What time? I have my radio interview at seven."

"When're you finished?"

"Probably around seven thirty, seven forty-five-ish."

"I'll pick you up from the radio station," he said. "Save you the trouble of calling a cab."

"Sure." It'd been almost three years since I'd gone bowling, so I would probably be rusty.

"Here's the studio's address," I said, showing him the piece of paper with the address that Al had given me. He took a picture of it with his phone.

"Sounds good. Just text me when you're done."

At 6:35 p.m., I was waiting outside when a yellow taxi pulled into the parking lot with the words Central City Taxi Company painted on it. I handed the driver my NJRA taxi pass and gave him the address for Central Radio Station.

I entered the studio building and was greeted by the receptionist. He led me to the broadcasting room, where Rob Grey sat in front of a microphone. Rob gestured for me to sit down in the empty chair across from him. I sat down, taking care not to bump the microphone in front of me.

"Welcome to Central Radio Sports Weekly on CRS-FM 101.5. My name is Rob Grey, and I'm your host. With me tonight is jet racer Jay Smith, the youngest qualifier for this year's National Jet Racing Association nationals. Hello, Jay."

"Hello, Rob." I felt my voice shake a little, knowing thousands of people were listening to me at that very moment.

Rob smiled encouragingly at me. He picked up a mug from his desk and took a sip from it. "All of us here at Central Radio would like to give a big thanks to you for joining us tonight."

"My pleasure." I couldn't think of anything else to say. After all, it was an honour to be on Rob's show.

"I've been following your career since you first joined Central City Jet Racing League last year. What's it like being the youngest pilot in this year's nationals, especially considering it's only your second year in the NJRA?"

"Well." I paused for a second. "I don't think age really matters. But back at training camp, when I flew solo for the first time, everyone was a bit shocked to see a little guy like me, I'm only five-five, flying so naturally."

"Do you ever feel you aren't taken seriously because of your age?"

"Sometimes I feel like I'm not taken seriously, but I don't know if it's because of my age. I don't know what it'd be like if I were older. After training camp, I was welcomed to Central City Jet Racing League with open arms, and it's a big reason why I am where I am now."

"Great to hear, Jay. I learn something new from everyone I talk to on the show. Is your family into aviation as well? Do they come to your races?"

"You see..." I tried to keep a straight face. I didn't want to be known as that guy who cried during his *Central Radio Sports Weekly* interview. "I have no connection to my birth family anymore, so I wouldn't know. My adoptive family doesn't care much for sports, although they supported my decision to join the NJRA."

"What inspired you to get into jet racing?"

"It all started when I lived at my first foster home, and there was an airport across the street. It was just a small airport, but I spent hours in front of the window watching all the planes taking off and landing. I was only four then, and it seemed like the coolest thing ever. I even told myself, 'Someday, I will fly a plane.'"

"And now your dream has come true. So your love of aviation started at a very young age."

"A few years later, I was moved to another home. I spent several years moving from home to home until I was adopted at the age of nine, but I'll never forget how I felt watching the planes. There's a certain feeling of freedom and living in the moment that comes with flying. What more can I say?"

"Sounds like you have some very fond memories. So what made you want to go to NJRA training camp?"

"I stumbled across a notice from the NJRA online. It said they were recruiting new pilots, no previous flying experience required. And, of course, no education requirements either."

"So you just had to jump on it, and you got accepted."

"It was like the best day ever when I got my acceptance letter for training camp. I mean, not only was it a chance to fulfill my childhood dream, but it was a decent job too. I didn't finish high school, so my only other options were factory work or construction. Now, two years later, here I am in the nationals."

"How are you feeling about next week, with Max Erikson having beaten you by mere milliseconds for first place at the West Coast Qualifier?"

"A bit nervous, but I'm confident I can redeem myself in the nationals."

"I see. And how do you feel about being up against Andrew Mayer, now that he's in the Central City League with you?"

"He can get on my nerves sometimes, but I try not to let it get to me."

"Do you usually prepare yourself mentally right before the race? Like, do you have any good luck rituals?" Rob asked.

"I'm not superstitious and definitely wouldn't do the whole Ash Christie pre-race prayers. If anything, I like to visualize the course before I even get onto the runway. Once I'm out there, I go with the flow."

"Do you think the key to winning is all in your mind?"

It can be. When it comes to manoeuvring around up there, sometimes you have to listen to the plane and get a feel for it."

"It's like you're the plane whisperer." Rob chuckled at

the end of that sentence.

"I guess so." *Plane whisperer, huh?*

Rob glanced at his watch. "So, Jay, before we bring this interview to an end, is there anyone you'd like to shout out to?"

"I'd like to thank Shauna Ritchie for all her support and Mike Jarrell at Central City for keeping my plane in tip-top shape at all times because things would literally be falling apart without him." I laughed out loud at my pun.

"Jay, it's been a pleasure having you on the show tonight. On behalf of Central Radio, we wish you all the best next week."

"Thanks."

Rob shook my hand.

"I know you'll be great," he whispered as he led me out of the recording room.

"Do you mind if I get a picture with you?" the receptionist asked me.

"Sure," I replied.

He picked up his tablet and took the picture.

"Thanks. It'll be going on our website."

I made my way out to the parking lot and texted Vinnie to let him know I was done. His black car pulled into the parking lot ten minutes later. He rolled down the window.

"Get in," he said. "Bowling alley's just around the corner."

"Didn't even know there was one around here." I shut the car door. "The only two bowling alleys I know about are on the other side of town."

"Yep, it's called Striker's Bowling. How was the interview?"

"Not bad. A bit emotional at times, but I was able to keep it together."

"That's good. They wanted me to do one too, but I felt like I wouldn't have much to say."

"You should have done it," I said.

"Maybe next time. I've never done a radio interview before. It sounds pretty intimidating." He stopped at a red light and adjusted the radio. It was set to the traffic station. "Public speaking was never really my forte."

"If you ever have the opportunity, go for it. Any interviews, be it newspapers, magazines, or TV. You're still early in your career, so it's a great way to build your fan base."

We arrived at a strip mall. There were barely any cars in the parking lot as all the stores had closed for the day. The windows of one store were boarded up and covered with graffiti. A couple of guys were shouting at each other in front of a car at the other end of the parking lot. A sign with the words "Striker's Bowling" painted in black block letters below a picture of a bowling pin stood on the sidewalk in front of a glass door. The door had metal bars attached to it.

Vinnie opened the door on the driver's side, but I hesitated. "Uh, Vinnie, are you sure you want to go here?"

"Why not? I was just here with Irene last week. She loves this place."

I had a feeling someone would jump out and grab me as soon as I opened my door, or we'd come out after we were done to find Vinnie's car all smashed up.

THE JET RACER

"Make sure you lock your car," I said, glancing around as I exited. "Just wondering why we didn't go to Riverview Bowl instead?"

I had never been to that place, but it looked much nicer than Striker's from the outside.

"Because this place has charm. You can't judge a book by its cover."

If his definition of charm is sketchy, that makes sense.

The heavy door creaked as Vinnie pushed it open. As I stepped inside, the smell of sweaty shoes and the clattering of bowling pins hit me. I followed Vinnie down a flight of dimly lit stairs, turning to look behind me every few seconds. The walls of the stairwell were covered in what looked like pencil scribbles. There were probably some sexual messages and images in the mix, but I was too preoccupied with watching my back to look closer.

The place was much smaller than the last bowling alley I'd been to. There were only ten lanes, and less than half were occupied. Most of the bowlers looked to be over the age of forty. The paint on the walls was yellowed and chipping. A shelf held several dull and dusty trophies. There was no arcade filled with pinball machines and racing games and no pub serving beer and wings.

A large banner on the wall behind the shoe rental counter caught my attention. It read, "Go Max #67". It was obvious who the owner would be cheering for in the nationals.

The smell of Lysol wafted through the air as we approached the counter.

We paid for two games; it was much cheaper than the last time I went bowling. A balding man in his late fifties handed us our scorecards, pencils, and bowling shoes. He wore a faded flannel shirt, and his breath smelled like cigarettes. The shoes were definitely showing their age. The coloured leather was all faded, and the stitching was coming loose.

"This is old-school bowling," Vinnie said, pointing at the scorecards with his pencil. "That's right. No electronic scorekeeping."

"Um, but don't you think," I hesitated, taking a moment to consider whether I should say it, "this place is a bit beat up?"

"I told you, it's got its charm." Vinnie smiled. "Plus, no whiny birthday party kids, no drunken frat boys. Cheap bowling, not to mention it's never crowded. What more could you ask for?"

I was surprised that cheap bowling was one of the reasons he preferred this dumpy place, given that Vinnie was usually not concerned about money. And what did Irene love about it? She was usually all about the nightlife.

We walked over to lane number ten and sat on the plastic chairs to change our shoes. The chairs creaked as we sat on them.

"You first," I said. Vinnie picked up the ball and bowled a strike.

"Nice one!" I shouted as he ran over to me. I gave him a high five. He marked an X on his scorecard.

The clattering of bowling pins surrounded me. I picked

up the ball, feeling the weight of it in my hand. My first roll was a gutter ball.

"Oops," I said, embarrassed. "Guess I am a bit rusty."

"Hey, don't sweat it," Vinnie replied. "It's not about the score; it's about having fun."

"You're right." I knocked down six pins with my next ball. I knew I couldn't keep up with him, but I pretended to be interested since he had invited me to hang out.

Vinnie showed me how to fill out the scorecard. Then, instead of getting up for his turn, he turned to me. "Hey Jay, do you mind if I ask something personal?"

"Sure, go ahead."

"Have you ever dated anyone before?"

"Not really; I guess I'm just not interested. Why do you ask?"

He got up and picked up his ball. "Just curious. I ended my last relationship last year."

"Was she not your type?"

"She was definitely my type," Vinnie explained. "We had known each other since high school and had a lot in common."

"That must have been tough. Was it hard to get over?"

"Not at all. We decided just to be friends."

He knocked down seven pins with the first ball. He hit the other three on the second for a spare.

I stood up for my turn to bowl. At least my first ball didn't end up in the gutter. I came close to a spare, except for that last pin that wouldn't fall over on the second roll.

"Not so rusty now, huh?" Vinnie said. I filled out my

scorecard. "So, no serious girlfriends?"

"I did go out with a girl back in high school for a very short time," I said.

"Did you not you like her?" He raised his eyebrows. "Or was there someone else?"

"Back then, I wondered if perhaps I liked boys more than girls."

He shrugged. "Either way, it makes no difference to me. It doesn't change who you are."

He waited for the guy in the next lane to bowl before staring down the lane with intense concentration. He bowled another strike.

"Yes! Go, Vinnie, go Vinnie!" he chanted, running toward me for another high five—way to rub it in.

"Vinnie picked up the pencil and recorded his score. "So, did you date any guys back in high school then?"

"No. I always thought something was wrong with me. But this morning, my old high school social worker told me I might be asexual. Before that, I never really knew what asexual meant, aside from what I learned in science class about how amoeba and plants reproduce."

"Very interesting. I don't think I'm asexual, but I don't get how everyone's so obsessed with sex and relationships. I don't think it's bad, but there's more to life than just that."

"I'm sure Max would disagree, though." I laughed.

"For sure." Vinnie smiled before laughing out loud with me. "But some people would rather be alone."

"Sometimes I think I spend too much time alone." Especially during my short-lived years of high school. Everyone around me was dating, and I couldn't have cared less. I never understood what was wrong with being alone, but my adoptive parents had given me the whole talk about not dating too young.

"Well, you're spending time here now," he replied.

I picked up the first ball for my third round, which ended with a spare.

"Do you go bowling a lot?" I asked, trying to change the subject while filling in my scorecard.

"Not really."

"You're pretty good, though."

Vinnie almost got another strike on his next turn, but one pin stubbornly remained standing. The pin fell over on the next ball, giving him a spare. As he sat down, the ceiling lights turned off and were replaced by the neon glow of black lights. A few of them were burned out. A disco ball shimmered, shooting streams of light over our heads. Vinnie's white t-shirt glowed under the black light; the brightly coloured bowling balls glowed too. I could feel the vibration of the bass in my body as rock music pounded throughout the sound system.

"This is like the best part," Vinnie said. "Cosmic bowling."

"I'm surprised such a run-down place like this even has cosmic bowling," I said.

Six more rounds went by, and our scorecards were full. Vinnie had won the game, just as I expected.

"My arm's getting tired," I said. "Let's take a break before the next game."

The guy in the flannel shirt from the rental counter

came up to our table with a plate of tortilla chips and salsa. "Snacks for you guys?"

"How much?" I asked. It was another surprise from that beat-up place.

"Always free during cosmic bowling," he replied, smiling as he put the plate on the table.

Vinnie picked up a chip and dipped it into the salsa. "So, reading anything interesting lately?"

"Just *Advanced Air Racing Strategies*," I replied.

"Weren't you reading that last month?"

"Doesn't hurt to reread it. The nationals are coming up fast, and I want to improve as much as I can before then."

"Can I borrow it when we get back? I could sure use some new strategies." He ate another chip. "If I'd stuck to plans, I probably wouldn't have been sixth last week."

"You should be proud that you made both the qualifier *and* the nationals as a rookie."

"What do you think the course will be like this time?" Vinnie asked.

"I'm not sure, to be honest." I grabbed a couple of chips from the plate. They change the course for every event and don't tell us what it would be until race day. There're no physical racetracks in the sky, so they can set the course as whatever they want. "It's all part of the challenge to see how well you can stay on course."

"For sure. Ready for some more bowling?"

CHAPTER 4

It was almost 10:30 p.m. when Vinnie and I returned from the bowling alley. I grabbed my toiletries bag from my nightstand drawer and went down the hallway to the bathroom. Vinnie was washing his face at one of the sinks.

"Shower's yours," he said, smiling. "You're not following me, are you?"

"Nope."

"Just messing with you." He laughed.

"That was fun tonight," I replied. Though half the time I only pretended to have a good time since I could barely bowl spares.

"We should go again," he said, turning off the tap and drying his face with a towel.

"Think Juli might want to come too?" I asked. "The more the merrier, right?"

"She might. I'll have to ask her." He yawned. "Anyways, I better hit the hay. Bowling tires me out every time."

"Alright, goodnight then."

He picked up his toiletries bag and left the bathroom. I

had a shower and put on a clean T-shirt and pyjama pants before brushing my teeth and washing my face. While drying my hair in front of the mirror, I noticed it had grown quite a bit; it reminded me of David Bowie. I turned around to check it out from different angles. I really liked how it looked. I returned to my room, turned off the lights, and climbed into bed. I was tired from bowling, but I still tossed and turned. Just as I was on the brink of falling asleep, the mental image of the student at Julianne's training camp masturbating in the training simulator seat crept back into my mind. I rubbed my face with the blanket, trying to get that icky feeling off my skin. Finally, my thoughts melted into the darkness as I drifted off to sleep.

"Morning, Jay. Here's your breakfast," Mike said, handing me my plate just as I returned to my room from the bathroom. "Can I get your logs from yesterday?"

I handed Mike my logs to be sent off to the NJRA.

"Found this in your garbage," he said, holding the magazine I had thrown out the day before. "Thought you might've tossed it by accident."

"No, um, Vinnie was hanging out in my room last night, and his allergies were acting up." My voice stuttered a bit as I lied. I didn't want to admit I had thrown it away because of the pictures of Max. "He asked if he could read it and then sneezed on it."

"If you don't mind, I'll take it. Why throw out a perfectly good magazine?" Mike tucked it under his arm. "Everything alright?"

I nodded. I guess the thought of touching, let alone

ANDY DAVIDS

reading, a magazine that had supposedly been sneezed on didn't gross him out. After all, he was our league caretaker, so he probably wasn't easily grossed out.

Mike gave me a doubtful look. "You look nervous."

"Just a little pre-nationals nerves. A bit anxious because it's my first time."

"It's all good," Mike replied, patting me on the back. "If anything, it only pushes you further. Don't sweat it too much."

"Do you know if Andrew's plane will be okay for the nationals?" I asked him.

"He sure belly-flopped it pretty hard. You should see the underside of that fuselage. Some of the wiring's damaged, too."

"Is it fixable?"

"We'll find out when I work on it today. The scratches and dents on the fuselage shouldn't be too hard to take care of. A few hours with some tools and paint should do it. But a good amount of wiring will probably need to be redone."

After Mike left, I looked out the window. It was raining. Not the best weather for practising, and nationals were only two days away.

I picked up *Fahrenheit 451* from the floor where I'd tossed it after finishing it the night before and put it back on my bookshelf. I needed a new book. I walked down the hallway to the leisure room, just past the lunchroom. Julianne and Irene were sitting at a table in the middle of the room playing Monopoly.

Andrew was sitting on the couch by himself, flipping

through an issue of Modern Pilot. He seemed to be skimming through it. It looked exactly like the one I had thrown out.

"I win!" Irene shouted triumphantly. Julianne groaned. The two of them packed up the game and stood up.

"We're heading into town for a bit," Irene said. "You two need anything?"

"I'm good," I replied.

Andrew looked up from the magazine. "Could you pick up some instant coffee? The stuff here is stale as hell."

"Sure," Julianne said. "See you in a bit."

"Want to play a game?" I asked Andrew, pointing to the shelf of board games.

"Not into games." He closed the magazine, holding the page with his finger, and looked up at me. I sat on the couch so I could get a look at the magazine. It was indeed the one I had thrown out.

"What're you looking at?" he scowled at me.

"Oh, nothing," I replied, trying to take my eyes off the magazine.

"If you're looking at this, Mike gave it to me," he said. "Said he found it in the trash. You read Modern Pilot too?"

"Yeah, I've been reading it since last year."

"My dad wrote quite a few articles for them." He took a closer look at me. "By the way, what's with your hair?"

He flicked the side of my hair with his free hand.

"What do you mean?" I pulled away from him. "Didn't say you could touch it."

"Going to cut it for the nationals?"

"Why? I like it. What does it matter to you?"

"Hope your headset cap still fits," he teased, rubbing the sides of his Ivy League haircut.

"Julianne's hair is even longer, and hers still fits." I could feel my face getting hot.

"Can't you take a joke?" Andrew said. "I'm just saying you should get a haircut. It'll look better, trust me."

"But Julianne doesn't look bad with long hair."

"Well, she's a girl," he argued. "You can't compare apples to oranges. You're a guy, right?"

"Yeah, but who decided that only girls and women should have long hair? Surely, everyone had long hair before haircuts were invented." It was something that had bothered me for a long time.

"Unless you're going Landon Rose on us now. You saw what she went through."

"Don't you mean he?"

"She can call herself Landon and dress like a guy, but she's still a lady." Andrew tossed the magazine on the floor beside the couch. "There're many different ways a lady can look. Just look around you."

"Maybe I'm like the male version of a tomboy. Tomgirl, I guess?"

"I believe the word you're looking for is *transvestite*." He cringed slightly.

"I like *tomgirl* more."

"Either way, you're a guy," he insisted. "But who am I to stop you if you're not?"

"I just want to be myself," I replied.

"Do I start calling you Jenny Smith now?"

"No, I'm still Jay."

I actually like the sound of the name Jenny.

"Think about this." He stood up and started pacing in front of the couch. "If I started calling myself Anna and went to races with fake boobs and a dress, you think anyone would watch me?"

"I would." I was starting to lose my patience. "I'm no less a fan of Landon since he came out."

"But that's you. What about everyone else?"

"You can't please everyone," I said.

"If I did that, it would hurt my fan base," he shot back. "That's what I'm trying to say."

"But I respect Landon because of what it took to go through all that, especially with the whole country watching."

"Jay, when you take the road less travelled, there is no knowing where you end up."

I was having a hard time absorbing everything he'd just said. I could not believe that people still felt that way.

"David Bowie was known for his gender-bending performances, and there were always people who didn't like him," I explained. "But he never let it stop him from being the way he was, like wearing dresses, colourful makeup, and sparkly bodysuits."

"Jay, don't tell me you're planning to show up in a dress at the nationals."

"I never said that. I'm just saying that I'm the male equivalent of a tomboy." I shook my head. This argument was getting nowhere. It was like arguing with my adoptive mom, who gave me a hard time whenever I showed an interest in anything that she considered feminine.

"Don't come crying to me when the pressure of the safety harness ruptures your Dolly Parton implants during a rough landing. Cleanup on aisle Eight Zero!"

I rolled my eyes at him. I really didn't know what to say to that.

"You see, everyone has fetishes, but fetishes are meant to be private," Andrew said.

"But it's not a fetish."

"Remember how people boycotted the NJRA over Landon?" Andrew explained. "Think of it this way. Planes have vertical stabilizers and wings for a reason."

"Yes." I sighed. I could see where this was going.

"You could design one without them. That doesn't mean it's a good idea."

"I get it, but some things change with time. Today, David Bowie wouldn't be considered as shocking as he was back in his day."

"Yes, but you can't change the fact that a plane without wings and vertical stabilizers isn't going to fly too well, right? Unless the laws of physics suddenly change."

I gave up arguing with him and walked away. He went back to reading the magazine, and I grabbed the remote from the bookshelf and turned on the TV. It was on the movie channel; Julianne must have been watching it before I arrived. I scrolled through several movie and music channels before selecting the hard rock channel. Metallica was playing.

"Would you turn that down, tranny boy?" Andrew whined. Then he stood up and walked into the hallway.

"Everybody, Jay's in the room and *it* won't let me read in peace."

That was the first time I'd ever had someone refer to me as *it*, or *tranny* for that matter, but I had a feeling it wouldn't be the last. I sat on the couch and went back to flipping through the channels. I wanted to leave Metallica on to piss Andrew off, but I didn't feel like listening to them anymore. After a couple of minutes of scrolling through the channels, I turned off the TV and went to the bookshelf to look for something to read.

I heard Max's voice. "Is he getting to you?"

I turned around. He was standing at the doorway.

"A bit," I replied. "What are you doing here?"

"I got something for you."

He handed me a parcel. The seal had been ripped open.

"Go ahead, look inside," he said.

I looked inside the envelope and saw a folded-up T-shirt. I pulled it out and gave it a shake to unfold it. It was a Tool shirt with artwork from the *10,000 Days* album on it.

"They sent the wrong size. I didn't want to bother sending it back," he explained. "Thought you'd like it."

"Thanks." *He knows me well, but why is he giving me a gift?*

"Had one like it years ago and wore it on the road with my band for several tours. It always brought me good vibes, so I wore it until it was full of holes."

"So you wanted to relive the memories by buying one?"

"Pretty much."

"Then why are you giving it to me? Don't you want to exchange it for one in your size?"

"Thought you could use a good-luck charm, like something to cheer you up when you're feeling down." Then Max smirked. "Maybe it'll cheer you up when you don't make first place at the nationals."

"Thanks," I said. "Though I don't think I'll need any cheering up."

"Sometimes, when I feel crappy, I go to my room, put on a song, and jam along on my bass, and that cheers me up," he said. "You've probably found your ways, given your life."

Max knew about my past. I guess I was lucky that I was pretty young when the worst of it happened. It meaning the day I was taken from my birth parents' home to the foster home; the social worker at the doorstep, handing me a garbage bag and telling me to put all my belongings into it before saying that I was 'leaving now.' It was a long time ago, but it still felt like yesterday.

"I like to read when I'm feeling down," I said. "At least reading's healthy. I never really got into video games or TV shows, so books just became my thing."

I turned back to the bookshelf.

"Wish I got through books at the rate you do," he said. "I have one you might enjoy."

"Yeah? What is it?" I was hoping he wasn't being sarcastic, only to hand me some kind of erotica, which I could not see myself enjoying.

"You like Iron Maiden, right?"

"I do, just haven't listened to them much lately."

"You know Bruce Dickinson, right?"

"Yeah, their singer."

"That guy used to be one of my biggest idols. He was the one that first got me interested in flying planes. Have you heard of his book *What Does This Button Do?* It's all about his childhood, his fight with cancer, and his competitive fencing career."

"Never heard of it, but I'd love to read it," I replied.

"It's in my room. Want to come with me to get it?"

I followed him to his room and waited for him in the hallway. He handed me the book, then looked toward the window in his room for a second. The sky had cleared up.

"Planning to fly today?" I asked. "It's nice out."

"Probably going to fly with Juli when she gets back," he replied.

"How do you know she wants to fly with you?" I said, remembering my conversation with Julianne the day before.

"That's none of your business." He changed the subject. "But I want to know why you spend so much time doing aerobatics?"

"Because they're fun. No other reason, really."

"And yet you haven't entered an aerobatic competition all season."

"I work on turns and handling-related stuff too, but sometimes you just have to let yourself go and do some flips and spins. But I'm not interested in competing in aerobatics."

"Being upside down isn't all that fun for me due to my high centre of gravity," Max said.

There he goes, talking about his height again. Was it a jab because I was shorter than him?

"Well, I'm going to fly now," I said. "Might as well take advantage of the clear skies. Thanks for the book."

I dropped the book off in my room and went to the hangar. I wondered what was up with Max and why he was suddenly being so nice to me. I tapped my key card on the reader and the heavy door slid open automatically. Upon entering, the first thing I noticed was a large piece of pink fabric wrapped around the fuselage of my #80 like a ballet tutu.

Andrew stood in front of his locker, putting away his flight jacket. "Thought I'd help you with a décor job before the nationals."

"Andrew, really?" I sighed.

"Too bad it's not aerodynamic," he teased.

I grabbed my flight jacket out of my locker and slammed the door. I pulled the tutu off my plane and tossed it toward the corner of the hangar. I couldn't help but wonder where he even got that thing from.

"What were you doing here?" I asked.

"Flying, what else?" He muttered, stomping his foot on the floor.

"Didn't you damage your plane?"

"Irene said I could use hers," he replied.

"What about for the nationals?"

"If you really need to know, Mike's arranged a loaner for me. Any more questions?"

I shook my head no. I did my pre-flight walk-around and checked to see if Andrew had done anything else to my plane other than give it that ridiculous tutu. Then I climbed into the cockpit and shut the canopy. I took a moment to enjoy the silence as I tried to clear my mind of Andrew. I needed to focus on working on my weak spots before the nationals.

"Jet Racer Eight Zero, avionics on," I said into my headset.

"Copy that," the air traffic controller responded.

I taxied out onto the runway.

"Jet Racer Eight Zero, requesting takeoff from runway two three."

"Jet Racer Eight Zero, you are clear for takeoff."

I taxied down the runway. I felt the ever-so-familiar force of the acceleration pushing me back against the seat as I lifted off. It was rare that I had the entire Central City Jet Racing League airspace to myself. I levelled myself with the horizon and pulled two barrel rolls in a row before heading upwards for a vertical loop. My loop was far from being as perfect as Andrew's, but he wasn't around to judge me, and neither was anyone else. I decided to try that climbing spin manoeuvre Andrew had been showing off. It did not go as well as I intended, but I knew I could eventually get it if I kept working on it.

I decided to work on my pylon turn technique. My turns weren't that bad, but it never hurts to practice. Because I was flying alone, I'd be able to focus better, and no fellow league members to watch and possibly judge me.

I tried to recall what I had read about pylon turns in *Advanced Jet Racing Strategies*. The first bit of information that came to my mind was to minimize movement when entering a fast turn. The author reasoned that this would create the least amount of drag on the plane. I used the hangar on the ground ahead of me as my turn centre and made my approach, mindful of not making too much movement or pulling back on the control stick. I had spent a lot of time working on turns but practising alone gave me a feeling of more significant achievement than I'd ever had before. I made a few more pylon turns around the hangar, focusing on the smoothness of the turn. I began to feel confident about the nationals.

Deciding to call it a day, I landed on the runway and taxied back to the hangar. I climbed out of the cockpit and wiped the sweat from my forehead. The cool breeze against my skin sent a pleasant shiver up my spine. It was 2:00 p.m., lunch time, although a bit late. I filled out my daily logs before going to the lunchroom.

Only Julianne and Irene were there. I sat down next to Irene. Julianne was looking at her laptop.

"Did you just get back?" I asked.

"We were back at 1:30, but the kitchen had just closed," Julianne said, glancing up at me.

"Doesn't really matter; we bought sushi," Irene added. She handed me an open take-out box of California rolls. "Have some."

Julianne held up a white plastic bag containing a box the same size as the one Irene gave me.

"This is for Mike," she said. "I'll bring it to him in a bit."

"How was your trip into town, aside from the sushi?" I asked.

"It was pretty good. For starters, I got a haircut," Irene said. She brushed the freshly trimmed sides of her hair with her fingers.

"It looks great."

"Thought I'd get it trimmed up before the nationals," Irene replied.

I went over to the water cooler to get a glass of water.

"Anything else interesting?" I asked as I sat back down.

"I did a rock climbing class with some of my fans, courtesy of a contest put on by one of my sponsors," Julianne said. "I'm all achy and exhausted now."

"I didn't know you were into rock climbing," I said. I took a bite of sushi.

"It's a new thing for me. I like how it keeps the stress away," Julianne replied. "I think they should build a climbing gym here."

"We all need to keep the stress away sometimes," I said.

"Flying itself isn't that stressful," Julianne explained. "But replying emails and keeping up with social media is."

I could only imagine, as she was the one who had to deal with fans writing to her about how they thought she was hot and all the things they wanted to do to her. I guess one privilege of being a guy was that I didn't have to receive that kind of attention all the time.

"It hasn't been too busy with social media for me," I said. "Just did a radio interview last night."

"Guess you can take it easy for a bit, then," Julianne replied.

"I'm doing a live video chat tomorrow morning," I said, taking a sip of water.

"You'll do great," Irene added.

"Vinnie and I went bowling last night, and there was a big Team Max banner behind the counter," I said. "And I've seen a bunch of graffiti for him around town. That's why I haven't gone into town much since the qualifier. Seeing all that support for him makes me more nervous about the nationals than I already am."

"I saw some banners in the windows in town with your name on them today," Irene said. "If it makes you feel better, I can assure you there were more Team Jay ones than Team Max."

It was nice to know that more of the locals were cheering for me instead of Max. But Max was going to visit the students at a local university's aviation program, and it didn't make me feel any better, knowing that he'd be busy getting all his fans there hyped up.

"Aside from the video chat, I guess I'll just be taking it easy tomorrow," I said. "I need a day without stress."

"We should both take it easy," Irene replied, looking at me sympathetically. "It's my second time at the nationals, and I still feel nervous."

"No plans for tomorrow?" I asked.

"I'll be in a chat with my family in San Francisco to catch up with them."

"Where did you and Vinnie go bowling last night?" Julianne asked. "That dumpy place in the strip mall, Striker's?"

"Yep, he kicked my ass at bowling, too," I replied.

"He's pretty good, alright, but he's yet to beat me." Irene laughed. She turned to Julianne, pretending to be offended.

"And by the way, Striker's isn't dumpy." Irene smiled at me. "Next time, I'll come along, and I can teach you a few tricks."

"Mad props to you two heading out there at night," Julianne said. "Especially after that drive-by shooting in the parking lot last week."

"It's not that bad," Irene replied. "You just have to be sensible. I've honestly felt less safe in downtown Spokane than there."

"Did you remember to pick up that instant coffee?" A voice was heard from the entrance of the lunch room. Andrew stood at the doorway with his arms crossed. I froze immediately, trying not to make further eye contact with him.

"Yes, there are two jars of it over there," Irene replied, pointing at the jars next to the hot water machine. He walked over to the coffee machine and picked up one of the jars.

"Why did you have to get the stupid Walmart brand stuff," he complained. "Anyone with at least half a brain wouldn't drink that shit."

"You didn't tell her what brand you wanted," I replied. "You just said to buy some instant coffee."

He turned around and left the lunch room without saying another word.

CHAPTER 5

Tool's "Parabola" played on my speakers as I sat on my bed, relaxing and enjoying the music. The sky was darker than usual for an August evening. Sitting on the chair across from my bed, Vinnie was reading my copy of *Advanced Jet Racing Strategies*, which I had lent him.

"You mind if I change the song?" he asked.

"Go for it."

He put the book down on the floor, open to the page where he'd left off. He walked over to my computer and clicked on the song "Ænema."

"It's been a while since I heard this one," he said. "Tried to learn it on guitar a while back, didn't get very far on it. I love that opening riff."

"To me, that's pretty good," I replied. "I have no musical skill unless you count pressing play on my playlists."

He smiled. "You're funny."

I could hear the pitter-patter of raindrops on the roof through the music. Water droplets ran down the window.

"Looks like the rain's picking up," I said, as the sound of the rain increased to heavy clattering.

"Wait, it's more than rain." Vinnie turned down the music slightly. "I think it's hail."

I looked out the window again.

"You're right," I said, turning back to Vinnie.

"You won't believe what Andrew did to my plane today."

"What'd he do?"

"He put a tutu on it," I said. Vinnie started laughing as soon as I said the word *tutu*. "So if you see a piece of pink fabric lying around in the hangar, that's what it is."

Vinnie laughed harder, so loud that Max could probably hear it from his room. I hoped he wouldn't come by to see what was going on.

"Uh, that's not funny," I said.

"I'm not laughing at you personally. You just caught me off guard."

There was a loud rumble outside.

"Wait, uh, was that thunder?" A sheet of white light flashed across a dark cloud in the sky as I looked over at the window. I started counting, but the rumble of thunder less than a second after shook the entire room. I could feel my heart beginning to pound. *Wow, that was close.*

"Vinnie, uh, uh, did you see that?" My voice trembled as I felt my breathing get heavy. I pointed to a large tree not far from my window. It was split down the middle and charred black.

"That was intense. You alright, Jay?"

"Ye... ye... yeah, I'm fine."

"It's just a little thunder and lightning. It'll pass. I grew up in Connecticut, and we'd get heavy storms like this in the middle of the night at this time of year."

"That doesn't sound fun." I paused. *Just a little thunder and lightning, just a little thunder and lightning.* "I can't believe I'm twenty-one, and, uh, I'm still scared of thunderstorms."

"It's normal to have fears. We all have them."

"Of all the things to be afraid of, why thunderstorms? Surely flying is much more dangerous."

"Everyone's afraid of something," Vinnie said. "I mean, I'm almost twenty-four, and mould still bothers me. It's like my biggest weakness."

He turned the music back up to help drown out the sound of rain pounding on the roof. I tried to focus on the music as opposed to the storm outside.

"I wasn't really nervous the first time I flew solo at training camp, but I wasn't a hundred percent calm either," Vinnie said. "I was more excited than scared."

"I was pretty nervous the first time I soloed, but then again, training camp was the first time I'd been on a plane my entire life."

"Really?" Vinnie's eyes widened. "You've never travelled with your parents?"

"We either drove or took the train. My dad had a fear of flying."

"So training camp must've been quite nerve-wracking and exciting simultaneously."

"Like I said, I was nervous, but I've never really been scared of flying."

A white fork of lightning flashed from the corner of a

large cloud. I got up from my bed and shut the curtains as I started counting again.

I let out a squeak of panic when the rumble of thunder came. Two seconds that time. At least it was moving away.

"Want to hear a funny story?"

"Uh, sure," I stuttered.

"When my sister and I were kids, she had this baby doll that would giggle and make baby sounds when you pretended to rock it to sleep."

"That sounds cute. I always wanted a baby doll, but my dad said they were for girls whenever I asked for one."

"Anyways, whenever one of those huge storms happened in the middle of the night, the vibration of the thunder would set the doll off."

"As much as I wanted a doll, I sure wouldn't want it going off in the middle of the night!" The thought of a doll giggling in the darkness was very creepy. Definitely not comforting like a doll was supposed to be.

"Even after she got rid of that doll, I swear I heard the giggles whenever there was a late-night thunderstorm."

"I blame my dad for my fear of thunderstorms. When I was little, he told me that lightning always hits the tallest object around, and there was this big tree right outside my window," I explained. "I used to sleep with a pillow over my head whenever the forecast said there was a risk of thunderstorms overnight so that it would muffle the sound and block out the light."

"That's very clever," Vinnie replied.

"I have to say, listening to music while waiting for the

storm to pass is much more enjoyable than putting a pillow over my head. And, of course, chatting with you."

The next morning, I checked myself out in the bathroom mirror after my shower. My hair was growing fast, but I certainly wasn't concerned that my headset cap wouldn't fit like Andrew had said.

After leaving the bathroom, I passed Mike and his breakfast cart outside Vinnie's door. He handed Vinnie a tray. It was oatmeal with toast. "I'll be right there with your breakfast," he told me.

Back in my room, Mike handed me my tray, and I gave him my logs from the day before. "How're you feeling about the nationals?" he asked.

"Not bad."

"Good to hear. Ya'll need to be at Westcoast Airsports Stadium in Utah County by ten tomorrow morning."

"What about Andrew since, well, he can't fly in?"

"They're sending a charter plane to pick us up."

"I take it he got a loaner?"

Mike nodded. "It's waiting for him at the stadium."

He went back to pushing the breakfast cart down the hall. I sat down at my desk and had a few spoonfuls of oatmeal. It wasn't bad; definitely a nice change from French toast. I opened the jam packet and spread some on my toast. As I was taking a bite, there was a knock on the door. I could tell it was Vinnie from the way he knocked.

"Come in."

"Morning, Jay," Vinnie said, opening the door. "You look tired. Get any sleep last night?"

"Yeah." I yawned. "I went to bed around midnight, just after you left. I was lying in bed for who knows how long after that storm was over before I fell asleep."

"Any plans for today?" Vinnie asked.

"Doing a live video chat in a bit," I replied.

"That'll be good for building your fan base," Vinnie said. "I'm going to my friend's birthday lunch this afternoon. Haven't seen him in a while."

"Have fun."

I finished breakfast and left the plate outside my door for Mike to pick up. Then I sat down at my computer. The NJRA organizes these video chat sessions to give pilots a chance to interact with their fans. I opened the official NJRA forum, signed on to the chat room, and enabled video chat. I waved at the webcam and said "hello" to everyone in the chat room. I read the messages as they scrolled by in the chat window.

TeamJayGurl: OMG its Jay!

1099858729: Want to get rich fast? Learn how you can make your first million from home today! Click on the link to learn how to take advantage of this limited-time offer!

xxJayFan8oxx: Hi Jay!

TeamJay4Ever: What will you be wearing?

Mark2010: why do you wanna know what he's wearing you perv

TeamJay4Ever: Like under your flight jacket?

Mark2010: his undies obviously

1099858729: Want to get rich fast? Learn how you can make your first million from home! Click on the link to learn how to take advantage of this limited-time offer!

(User 1099858729 has been removed from the chat room—
ADMIN)

SmithNumber80: you really need a haircut

TeamJayGurl: no it's cute I like it

"Uh, thanks TeamJayGurl." I felt myself blushing.

TeamJay_or_bust: i hear erikson sleeps with illegal aliens

Averageguy_54: Erikson for gold!

xxJayFan30xx: Erikson sleeps with officials

SmithNumber80: Max Erikson murders kittens

ItsEmmy: my dog likes to hump Erikson's legs

TeamJay_or_bust: shut up

ItsEmmy: Err-dick-son

LeannaNumber80: OMG will you be at the meet and greet table? Can you sign my butt?

"I'll be there," I said, "though I don't know about signing your butt. Look forward to seeing you." Her butt would definitely take the cake for the oddest item I'd ever signed.

LeannaNumber80: Yay!

80Fan4Lyfe: hey Jay will you sign my face?

"Sure, if you come to the meet-and-greet table." First a butt, and then a face. I hoped they were joking so I wouldn't have to sign either.

GoVinnie37: so you'll never wash your face again?

80Fan4Lyfe: yeah if Jay signs it

GoVinnie37: ewwww you nasty!

"We've got free posters at the table." Hopefully Leanna, if that was even her real name, would decide to pick up one of those instead of asking me to sign her butt.

Gamerdood: i heard Erikson punts babies over the Mexican border!
ItsEmmy: i heard Gamerdood picks his nose
GuyfromWY17: Screw Jay! Ash Christie for gold!
GuyFromNewYork: Jay can you tell Julianne Madison to marry

I wasn't sure whether I should respond to that, but I guess it was a good thing I didn't.

Chris1995: No she's mine!

I didn't bother to answer. I had no doubt that Julianne always got comments like that, just like she'd told me about female jet racers having to deal with all sorts of crap like that.

TheJetGuy: How do you feel about the fact that Erikson beat you in the west coast qualifier?
Gamerdood: yeah why did you let that baby punter pass you?

"I don't think I did that bad, but he definitely made some moves I didn't see coming. I am still disappointed, but I'll learn from my mistakes and know to play my cards a bit differently this time."

TheJetGuy: You moved too much on that final turn.

"I thought I was far enough ahead of him. My eye was on the finish line, almost like tunnel vision. But he reacted to that last turn much smoother than I did and caught up to me."

There's a backseat driver, or rather, a backseat pilot, in every bunch, I thought to myself, then laughed at my own joke. I tried to explain what had happened, trying to hide my frustration.

NJRAfan: That's why Erikson's talking to my son at his flight school today instead of you. He wants to join the NJRA someday and he sure knows who he'll be cheering for!

"Well, I wish your son the best, NJRAfan." *Way to rub it in, NJRAfan.*

TeamJay4Ever: I saw you just signed a deal with Richards Aero Specialists
GoVinnie37: too bad about what happened with your previous sponsor

"It's alright. I'd had a feeling for some time that they were going to drop me for Erikson. At least Richards isn't going to drop me anytime soon."

LeannaNumber80: Jay should get sponsored by Pizza Hut!
TheJetGuy: who do you think will win the nationals this year if it isn't you or Erikson?

"Of course, Erikson's always the fast one, but Mayer's got a chance too. I'd say it'll probably be someone from the Central City League, considering five out of the twenty racers are from here. It's a tough call, but if it isn't me, Erikson, or Mayer, I'd say Giaconia's got a chance."

LeannaNumber80: I see your money's on Vinnie the rookie.

THE JET RACER

"He's only been with the NJRA for a year, but the fact that he qualified for the nationals so early in his career shows he's got potential. I've flown with him several times, so I know what he's capable of. It seems like everyone who's made it to the nationals as a rookie does pretty well." *Besides, he and I are pretty good friends.*

ILiketoFly: what about Irene Chan?

"Perhaps. I think her biggest weakness is her turn technique. She tends to make bigger movements, which slow her down. But she made up for it when she took home first in the West Coast Championships earlier this season."

Averageguy_54: which was like the biggest fluke ever...
TeamJay_or_bust: ewww
TeamJay4Ever: all because Erikson's engine crapped out

"I still think she could've made it to first place even without that fluke," I said.

TeamJay_or_bust: i'm not cheering for that ugly dyke
GuyFromNewYork: What's with all the homophobia?

Typical chat room bullshit. I knew there was no point in arguing with people like that online.

Chris1995: only a matter of time before she pulls a Landon Rose...
ILiketoFly: TeamJay_or_bust started it everyone report him
(User TeamJay_or_bust has been removed from the chat room - ADMIN)
NJRAfan: You know who my son and I are cheering for, Jay.
Bass_man117: Better Madison than Chan, at least she's hot

84

GoVinnie37: rumour says she's getting implants for next season

NJRAfan: Then the sponsors will just come pouring in like crazy

"It's tough for me to say who will win." I tried to steer the conversation back to the nationals. "There are just so many factors at play. It's like asking me to predict the weather or something."

LeannaNumber80: at least it'll be clear skies all week

Gamerdood: perfect for punting babies

ItsEmmy: and picking your nose if youre the person above

"They couldn't have picked a better day for the nationals. Anyways, I got to run now, and it was great chatting with all of you. For those who won't be at the stadium, don't forget to tune in to ESPN at 3:00 p.m. Pacific Time!"

LeannaNumber80: Can't wait to meet you!

ItsEmmy: good luck Jay!

I sighed as I signed out of the chat system and closed the web browser. I shut my computer down and decided to go to the leisure room to relax and get my mind off everything I had to put up with during that chat. *As if my stress about the nationals isn't enough.*

It was an hour before lunchtime. Irene and Vinnie were watching TV when I got to the leisure room. It was on the movie channel.

"We're just watching *Interstellar* right now. Feel free to join us," Vinnie said.

"Never seen it before," I replied. "Is it good?"

"Yeah, it is. I've seen it many times, and I still enjoy it."

"It's one of those movies that sort of make you think," Irene added.

Coming in partway through the movie, I was confused by everything happening. And I wasn't much of a science person, unlike Vinnie. Unable to keep up with the storyline, I glanced out the window several times. I felt like flying, but I had already decided I wouldn't fly that day, as I didn't want to get myself too worked up before the nationals.

"What did you think?" Irene asked. The movie had ended.

"Really enjoyed it," I responded, snapping out of my thoughts. "Though it's safe to say quantum physics isn't my thing."

"I might go to the hangar to clean off my plane. Want to come along?" Irene asked us.

"Isn't Mike doing that?" Vinnie asked.

"Probably, but I'm sure he could use a hand," she said. "He's got a lot to do, taking care of all the mechanical stuff for five planes."

"You have a point," I said. I had planned to return to my room and start reading that Bruce Dickinson book, but giving Mike a hand sounded like a better idea. After all, the poor guy always had to do so much for us, even with his bad back. "Let's go."

Vinnie and I followed Irene to the hangar. Andrew stopped us in the hallway outside the electronic security door.

"Going out to fly?" he asked.

"Nah, just thought we'd go and clean our planes,"

Irene responded.

"Looks like it's already been done," he said. "Mike was working on that for the last few hours."

"What are you doing here?" Vinnie asked. "Didn't you wreck your plane?"

"Left my logbook in my locker."

"I see," I replied. "Where's Mike now?"

"He left a few minutes ago. His sister's visiting from Texas, and it's her last day here," Andrew said, tapping his key card on the reader. The electronic door slid open. "He's probably taking her to a nice restaurant for lunch."

He opened his locker, grabbed his logbook, and slammed the door. "Any more questions?" he grumbled before leaving the hangar.

I looked at Vinnie and Irene, eyebrows raised.

"Just remembered that I left my logbook in my locker too." Irene walked over to the lockers.

"Is that what he put on your plane?" Vinnie said. He was pointing at the crumpled piece of pink fabric on the floor. It was covered in dust, probably from Mike sweeping the floor.

"Yes. Now can we get rid of it?"

"Where the hell did he get it?" Vinnie picked up the fabric and examined it before tossing it into my arms. Just touching it made me feel the burn of tears in my eyes. I could hear Irene giggling as I crammed it into the garbage can.

"I get it now," she said.

"Hey, that's not funny," I said. My eyes widened. "Wait, what? What did you get?"

"The tutu plane, Andrew posted about it on the official forums," Irene responded. "I saw it earlier this morning."

"You've got to be kidding," I replied. "Nobody said anything about it during the live chat I just did."

"Maybe he posted it around that time, so they wouldn't have seen it yet. It's probably all over the unofficial NJRA sites, too," Irene said.

I pretended not to be bothered by it all.

"Well, I'm going back to my room to read for a bit," Irene said. "You two up to anything?"

"I'm heading into town for lunch with a friend," Vinnie said. "I'll catch you guys later."

"If you don't mind, could I catch a ride to that pizza place on Kelsey Avenue?" I didn't want to eat in the lunchroom with Andrew, let alone see him for the next few hours.

"I know which one you mean," he said. "The one nobody really goes to, right?"

"I guess nobody but me now." I just wanted to eat alone. I'd planned to spend the last few days before nationals relaxing, but Andrew's joke and the news of it spreading around the internet made that impossible. I knew that pizza place well. It had been the usual hangout for me and some high-school classmates when we wanted an "extended lunch break," as Ms. Ritchie had called it.

"Enjoy your pizza then," Irene said.

"Just have to grab something from my room first," I said to Vinnie.

"Okay. Meet you in the parking lot."

I went back to my room to grab the Bruce Dickinson book. I thought I could get a start on it while I had some time to myself, away from the airfield.

The highways, crossed by the occasional overpass, seemed to stretch on forever, but the fact that Vinnie's car had satellite radio set to the hard rock station made the time go faster. I lost myself in the music, letting it drown out the echo of Irene's laughter and Andrew's taunting in my head.

"I may be a rookie, but it doesn't take much to know that all that gossip is just a bunch of bullshit." Vinnie's voice snapped me back to reality. "Don't let it get to you."

"Don't worry. I won't."

"Trust me. I used to have friends who were really into all that."

"So did I, back in high school. Feels like forever ago."

"They'd be checking six different sources just to read about how so and so gained five pounds, who's going out with that girl, and whatnot."

"I'm sure there are true fans that actually want to follow my racing career."

He pulled over in front of Roman's Pizza on Kelsey Avenue.

"See you in a bit," he said. He waved at me before driving off.

The restaurant was quiet, except for the news station faintly playing on an out-of-tune radio and the sound of someone chopping vegetables. Just as I had expected, it was deserted. At least there were no Team Jay or Team Max references in the vicinity. I guess this part of town just wasn't into the spirit of the competition.

I was hit by nostalgia as I walked up to the counter. There was a very comfortable atmosphere inside the restaurant. Roman, the owner, stood behind the display case.

"What can I get for you?" he asked in his familiar Russian accent. His hair had gotten greyer over the years. "It's buy one slice get one half off right now, just so you know."

I didn't remember ever seeing him taking orders, but he was the only person there other than me. I looked into the glass case. It held the same kinds of pizza it always had; pepperoni, Hawaiian, Italian, vegetarian, and cheese.

"I'll just take two pepperoni slices."

"Any drink with that?"

"I'll get an iced tea. By the way, did the girl who used to work here like seven years ago quit?"

"That's Alina, my daughter. She got married a while ago, and now she's busy raising a family of her own." Roman put the slices on a paper plate before opening the drink cooler to get a can of iced tea.

"What about the guy?"

"That would be Charlie you're thinking of. He worked here for several years. Last I heard from him, he was moving to Arizona for university. Now that business is so slow, I'm considering selling this place."

I sat at the corner table where my classmates and I always sat. It felt almost strange to be eating at Roman's Pizza by myself. No obnoxious chatting and inappropriate jokes being thrown around, not that I missed any of that.

I wasn't surprised that Roman didn't remember me

from hanging out there all those years ago. For sure, I changed a lot since then. But I was surprised that he didn't recognize me from the NJRA. He probably didn't even watch TV, let alone follow NJRA.

As I ate, I read the book, taking care not to get grease or pizza sauce on the pages. As it always had been for me, reading was an escape. It was a relief to be alone, away from the airfield and Andrew's attitude.

CHAPTER 6

It was late in the evening and I had just finished playing a couple games of Trivial Pursuit with Vinnie and Irene in the leisure room. I passed Max's room on the way back to mine. His door was open, meaning that he wasn't on a video call with his daughter, or with anyone for that matter. I looked in the door. He was sitting on his bed reading an issue of *Sports Illustrated*.

"How did the workshop go?" I asked.

Excellent," Max said with confidence. "I asked them who they're cheering for. One guess what their answer was."

"Me?" I replied, sarcastically.

"They all shouted my name together. If that doesn't tell you something, I don't know what does. By the way, digging the new livery you got going on."

"What do you mean?"

"The ballerina plane," he said. He smirked as he carefully tore a page from the magazine.

"What're you ripping out?" I asked.

"Have a look yourself."

He turned the page in his hands toward me. It was a

THE JET RACER

picture of Julianne standing against the wall of a hangar. She was wearing her slightly worn-out pilot boots. Her orange and yellow flight jacket was unzipped, clearly displaying her cleavage. Her thick brown hair was down and her eyes were surrounded by heavy makeup. The words *Julianne 'The Phoenix' Madison, #10* were printed in white lettering in the lower right corner of the page.

I raised an eyebrow.

"Hey, it's a tasteful photo." Max protested. "Very artistic too."

"When was that even taken?" I asked.

"Couple weeks ago. It's definitely going to be in next year's NJRA calendar."

"It's so disgusting how much they pay her just to take off her clothes. Us guys don't have to deal with any of that."

"You're not accusing me of hating women now, are you?" Max shot back. "Just because I look at half-naked chicks?"

"I never said you hate women."

"Good, because I don't. I love my women, especially when they're good in bed."

"Just saying, because Irene complained about how degraded she felt after a photoshoot a while back," I explained.

Max sighed. "She looked a little uncomfortable in that bikini, but it's all about the money at the end of the day."

"Uh, yeah. I can't even imagine her wearing a bikini in real life," I said.

"That feminist dyke needs to stop bitching and

moaning. Men have been checking out ladies since the dawn of time," he complained. "I hate feminists."

"So would you still stare at that photo if it was Irene instead?" I asked.

"Yeah, especially if it was her *and* Julianne. If there's anything Irene and I can both agree on, it's that pussy is great."

I could feel my skin crawling at that remark. "Well, I don't read those magazines."

"You read what you want, I read what I want," he said.

You read that? I thought. *More like flipping through it and staring at all the pretty pictures.*

"Guess so," I said, wanting to end the conversation. "I'm going to bed. Busy day tomorrow."

I shut his door and went on to my room. It felt like another David Bowie kind of night. I put on *The Rise and Fall of Ziggy Stardust and The Spiders from Mars.* I sat down on my bed and made myself comfortable before picking up the Bruce Dickinson book trying to distract myself after that conversation with Max. It seemed like I was reading for an hour before I put the book down and decided it was time to sleep.

"Good morning," Vinnie said to my reflection in the corner of the bathroom mirror as I stood in the bathroom doorway. He put his toothbrush back in his toiletries kit and wiped his face with his towel. "Sleep well?"

"Pretty well."

"At least there weren't any thunderstorms to keep you

awake." He smirked.

"That's for sure." I had a feeling he would be bringing this up for a while.

"Do you want your book back?" Vinnie asked. "I'm finished with it."

"You're a fast reader."

"Nah, didn't read all of it. Just read most of the important stuff like all the tips on turns."

"You should read the whole thing," I said. "I don't need it back right now."

"Okay, thanks." Vinnie grabbed his towel and toiletries kit. "See you later."

I checked myself out in the mirror as I brushed my teeth. I could definitely see why that fan had told me me I needed a haircut, but I was really starting to like the look. I packed up my toiletries kit and returned to my room to get dressed. I placed my clothes for the next three days into my suitcase along with some books to read in my free time. I made sure to pack the Tool shirt Max had given me, as it was going to be my good luck shirt, at least for the nationals.

I went down the hallway to the lunchroom, rolling my suitcase behind me. There was nobody in the kitchen or in the lunchroom. Max was just leaving.

"Hope you remembered to pack your lucky shirt," he said, snickering. I could tell that he was teasing me. "You're going to need it."

I hurried toward the hangar, clutching a couple pieces of buttered toast in my free hand. I tossed my suitcase into the cargo compartment of #80 and climbed into the cockpit. I did my pre-flight check.

"Jet Racer Eight Zero, requesting takeoff from runway two-three."

"Tower to Jet Racer Eight Zero, you are clear for takeoff. Best of luck at the nationals tomorrow!"

Two hours of flying later, an air traffic controller directed me along the runway as I arrived at Westcoast Airsports Stadium. After taxiing into the pit area, I climbed out of the cockpit and was greeted by two members of the stadium's pit crew.

"Welcome!" They said together. The taller one on the left pointed toward a long table.

"Registration's that way."

I saw Max, Irene, and Vinnie already lined up to register. I stood behind Vinnie as I waited for my turn.

"This stadium's so much nicer than the one in Reno, don't you think?" Vinnie said.

"Definitely," I replied. "They should've held the qualifier here."

I guess they wanted to save the nicer stadium for the bigger event. I couldn't help but wonder what the stadiums where they hold the World Series of Jet Racing were like.

"Look at the size of those grandstands," Vinnie added.

The grandstands, empty now, were almost twice the size of the ones back at the Reno stadium. A large TV screen for the spectators, also bigger than the one in Reno, took up an entire wall across from the grandstands.

"I know," I replied. "It's pretty impressive."

Vinnie finished registering. It was my turn. I stepped up

to the desk like I had done at every other race.

"Jay Smith, Central City Jet Racing League," I said to the official as I handed him my NJRA ID card. He put a check mark next to my name on the list of twenty racers' names. Then, he handed me my ID back along with a blue card with my name and NJRA member number on it.

"Here's your key card. It's for access to the hangars as well as the racers' building. We use an RFID reader here, so you just need to hold it up to the scanner for three seconds," he explained as I took both of the cards from him.

"Thanks."

"If you want to drop off your stuff, the men's sleeping quarters are just down the hallway once you get into the racers' building. The spa will be open in an hour so you can enjoy complementary facials and hot stone massages, or just relax in the hot tub."

"Sounds good."

I found my way to the men's sleeping quarters and chose my bed for the next three days. Max's flight jacket was on the bed in the far right corner of the room. Unlike the sleeping quarters in Reno, the paint on the walls here wasn't turning yellow and chipping off. I put my suitcase under the bed. Vinnie walked in and took the bed next to mine.

"I can't believe what just happened," he said, stuffing his suitcase under the bed. His face was a little red.

I sure hoped it wasn't related to the whole tutu plane incident.

"They had to get security to let me in," he said. "My key card wouldn't open the front door."

I frowned. "That's odd. Mine worked fine."

"I didn't hold it up to the scanner long enough," he explained, slapping his forehead and laughing.

"Well, now you know."

"Going for lunch?" he asked. "I wonder what's on the menu."

We walked to the dining hall, down another hallway and around the corner from the entrance to the racers' building. There were several tables with actual chairs, unlike the cafeteria tables back at the league airfield. And the tables were much newer than the ones in the dining hall at the Reno stadium, and not covered with food stains that had been there for who knows how long.

The food selection was simple, but appetizing. Plates filled with sandwiches on them cut into little triangles and held together with toothpicks caught my eye. Next to each plate was a paper sign saying what kind of sandwiches it held. I decided to go with the smoked chicken and avocado wrap and a cup of English breakfast tea. As I sat next to Vinnie and Mike at the table with everyone else from Central City, I tried to avoid eye contact with Andrew.

"How're you feeling about tomorrow?" Mike asked.

"Trying not to think about it too much," I replied.

"I think I should be more nervous than you," Vinnie said.

"If anyone should be nervous, it should be me," Julianne added from the far end of the table. She looked a bit uncomfortable sitting across from Max, but it seemed like they were having an alright conversation otherwise.

"No need to be nervous," Mike said. He patted me on the back. "What do you think of the food so far?"

"These wraps are really good. Any idea what's for dinner?" I asked, taking a sip of my tea.

"It's pizza night," Mike replied.

"Will there be anything else?" I asked, remembering that I just had pizza a day ago.

"Probably salad," Andrew said. I was still trying to avoid looking at him. "I'm sure you can live on rabbit food."

I made my way back to the men's sleeping quarters after lunch, thinking I should get my log for the flight from Central City Airfield done before I forgot. After that, a nap sounded very appealing. I pulled my suitcase out from under the bed and took out my logbook along with a pen and my laptop to use as a writing surface. Just as I sat on the bed and flipped open the logbook to a new page, Vinnie walked into the room.

He sat down on his bed and bounced up and down on the mattress. "Yeah, these beds are really comfy."

"At least we won't be waking up with sore necks, like we did in Reno," I said.

He stood up and walked to the doorway. "Coming to the nationals kickoff after dinner?"

"Nah, I'm not a party person." I was planning to spend the evening reading more of that Dickinson book, and possibly getting started on one of the other books I had brought with me.

"But there's going to be karaoke."

"Don't like singing," I grumbled. If I wanted to listen to

music, I could just do it on my laptop.

"I'm not a good singer, but the whole point of karaoke is having fun. Give it a try," he said. "Or are pre-race nerves getting to you, Jay?"

"Not really," I replied. I didn't know why I hesitated to admit that I was nervous, given the fact that I'd already had much more personal conversations with Vinnie. Maybe it was because he looked up to me as a racer.

"You don't have to sing. You can just dance. It'll get your mind off things."

"I actually can't dance," I said, thinking back to all the times that I'd made a fool of myself trying to dance. I could sway back and forth out of beat, but that was about it. I could not help but laugh at myself inside my head. As much as I knew that Vinnie wanted me to go so that he could spend time with me, I just wanted to spend the night with some peace and quiet and my books.

"Heh, I'm pretty clumsy too," he replied. "But it's not every day you get to dance under the stars on a runway with loud music and lasers and disco lights."

"They sure put a lot of work into this, that's for sure."

"Of course, it's the nationals! And there's going to be a giant Twister game on the dance floor after karaoke."

"I'll see," I said. "But right now, I'm going to start on my logs."

"Catch you in a bit. I'm going to the leisure room."

I finished filling out my logs and tore the page out from the logbook. I slipped the page behind the front cover of the logbook to keep it safe until I had a chance to give it to Mike, and then put the logbook and laptop back into my suitcase. I set the alarm on my phone to wake me in an hour and I lay back on the bed. Just as I started drifting off to sleep, Max walked into the room. He said nothing to me as he passed by my bed on the way to his. Despite his presence, I could feel myself falling asleep without hesitation. It had been a long morning.

It was just after dinner and everyone else was making their way out to the runway for the kickoff party. They were all walking in groups, chatting, and laughing. Some of them had glow sticks around their necks and wrists while others were dressed in neon colours. They were really getting into the party spirit. Although I'd told Vinnie and Julianne at dinnertime that I would see them out there, I was debating whether I would go or not. I went back to the men's sleeping quarters and flipped open my book. I tried to focus on reading despite the constant thumping of the sound system outside. After two chapters, I gave up and stuck my bookmark in my book.

I decided to check out the leisure room just to see what it was like. I walked down the hallway, passing the women's sleeping quarters along the way. The thumping of club music echoed in the hallway like someone shouting in an empty underground parking lot. The heavy bass seemed much quieter in the leisure room.

I sat down on the couch and turned on the TV. I spent a few minutes flipping through the channels but nothing caught my interest. I left the leisure room and walked back down the hallway toward the exit of the racers' building. I paced around in circles in front of the door as the music thumped. Hesitantly, I pushed the door open. I told myself that I would only go say hi to Vinnie and Irene and then try to sneak away. As I stepped outside, I felt the warm summer evening breeze on my face. I could feel the vibration of the bass in my head as I got closer to the runway. Barricades wrapped in red, white, and blue Christmas lights formed a large square area on the runway, with security guards standing at each corner. Colourful stage lights surrounded the DJ booth at the end of the runway closest to the grandstands, with the rest of the sectioned-off square serving as the dance floor. At one corner, there was a long lineup for the bar, and on the opposite side, a lineup for the photo booth. I'd never understood the popularity of photo booths, since cameras had been standard on cellphones for years. The faces in the crowd were barely recognizable under the glow of the coloured lights and the fog machines.

My heart raced as I approached the crowd, hoping I didn't get lost in there before I could find Julianne and Vinnie and the others from Central City. The thumping of the bass was starting to make my head hurt.

I took a deep breath and walked onto the dance floor, past the security guards in their yellow safety vests. I wound my way through the crowd, looking for familiar faces. The DJ was playing some electronic music that featured a female singer. I didn't recognize the song, but from what I could make of the lyrics, it was about a girl longing for her lover, like so many other songs out there. I continued peering through the crowd, and finally saw someone familiar closer to the DJ booth. It was Max; he was so easy to spot, being the tallest person on the dance floor. As I got closer, I recognized the person next to him as Julianne. They were holding hands.

Julianne was wearing a blue sleeveless satin dress and silver heels. I was in jeans and a T-shirt. Then again, nobody had specifically mentioned formal dress.

"Jay, Jay!" I heard a shout from nearby over the music. I turned my head left and right, but couldn't pinpoint where it came from. The music soon became more upbeat. People began jumping up and down to the steady beat, making it hard for me to look around.

Then I heard a different voice. "Jay, over here!"

Someone grabbed my arm. I turned around.

"Hey Vinnie!" I shouted. I felt a bit calmer than I was before. Irene was standing next to him. Fortunately, Andrew was nowhere to be seen, probably buried in the crowd somewhere.

"I'm so glad you decided to join us," she said, grinning from ear to ear.

"Yeah, I managed to drag myself out." My face was sweating.

"Having fun yet?" Vinnie asked.

"Just got here," I replied.

"Are you going to dance?" Irene asked.

Here we go again with the dancing.

"I uh, don't dance."

"Heh neither does Vinnie," Irene replied, grabbing him lightly on the arm.

"At least I haven't tripped on my own feet!" Vinnie

said. "Your turn, Jay."

"I just said I don't know how to dance." I was ready to leave the party right about then. I began thinking of excuses to leave.

"Just start by jumping up and down," Irene said to me, grabbing my hand and interrupting my train of thought. "You've never danced under the stars like this, have you?"

I shook my head no. I had never been to an outdoor party like this before. I'd never even set foot in a nightclub, even though I'd turned twenty-one in February.

Max and Julianne were dancing together near the DJ booth, still holding hands. It was obvious how uncomfortable Julianne was feeling from how she was looking around every few seconds. I bet she really wanted to dance alone. I wanted to say something about it to Irene and Vinnie, but at the same time, it didn't feel right to talk about it. Julianne had her own boundaries and Max had been overstepping them many times, but I didn't want to gossip.

Instead, I turned to Irene. "Didn't know Max liked this kind of music."

I was hoping to spark a conversation about Max getting so close to Julianne. In all seriousness, I couldn't remember Max ever being into electronic dance music. But Irene was too into dancing to pick up on what I'd said.

I tried to jump up and down to the beat, but my sense of rhythm was as bad as it ever was. Max, on the other hand, was dancing perfectly in time to the beat, thanks to the fact that he used to be a musician.

"Now put your hands up and wave them," Irene

shouted. "You too, Vinnie."

"Everybody having a good time?" the DJ said into the sound system. The crowd cheered back in unison.

The DJ threw several beach balls into the crowd. One flew over my head and I tried to jump up to hit it, but not even the tips of my fingers got close. Vinnie reached up and easily caught the ball. He tossed it back into the crowd.

"Things are about to get bubbly out here!" the DJ announced. The crowd cheered again. He pushed a button on his station, turning on the bubble machines around the booth. The crowd waved their hands, trying to pop the bubbles. I guess bubbles always brought out everyone's inner child. I jumped up and down and waved my hands in the air, but the bubbles were out of reach, just like the beach balls.

I gave up and continued to jump up and down, finally finding myself in the zone with the music. It was as if the sheer number of people around me didn't matter anymore. I waved my arms in the air like I was fan cheering in the grandstands. I felt every thump of bass through my body, as if I had become a part of the music.

"Who's ready for some karaoke?" the DJ asked, turning down the music. The crowd cheered even louder than they did before. "Let's get those singing voices warmed up! Who's up first?"

Joe, a racer from Nevada that I'd met at the qualifier, ran up to the DJ booth.

"What's your name, young man and where are you from? What would you like to sing?" he asked, handing the microphone to Joe.

"I'm Joe from Desert Jet Racing League and I'll be singing *Don't Stop Believin'*." Joe gave the microphone back to the DJ.

That song is over forty years old, I thought. *There are so many newer songs out there he could be singing.*

"Alright everybody, give it up for our first singer of the night, Joe!"

The DJ handed the microphone back to Joe and cued up the song on his laptop. The lyrics were displayed on a blue background on the two TV screens, one on each side of the DJ booth.

Joe sang loudly. His voice was cracking, but the crowd didn't seem to care. They clapped and cheered when he was finished.

"I'll be back. Going to get a drink," Irene said.

Vinnie nudged my arm. "Your turn, Jay."

There was no way I could get up there and sing in front of everyone. I really needed to get out of there fast. I'd reached the point I did at every other party I'd been to, thinking about how to break away without sounding rude.

"I don't think they have any songs I know how to sing," I said.

"You could just sing *Don't Stop Believin'* again," he replied. "Everyone knows that."

"I've got to go now, I'm tired." I forced a yawn.

"Leaving already?" Vinnie nagged, looking at his watch. "You're going to miss the Twister game!"

"The music's starting to give me a headache."

"But you were having so much fun a minute ago."

"I'm partied out." I yawned again, rubbing my eyes.

Vinnie sighed. I waved goodbye to him as I walked away from the crowd. I passed the bar, but I didn't see Irene waiting in line. I looked around and spotted her going into the photo booth on the other side of the square.

Back at the racers' building, I grabbed my toiletries kit and went to brush my teeth. I could feel my heart rate returning to normal as I entered the peace and quiet of the bathroom. I returned to the sleeping quarters and crawled into my bed. But it was only 11:45 p.m., and despite saying I was tired earlier, I didn't really feel like sleeping yet.

My phone beeped, breaking the relative silence of the sleeping quarters. It was a text from Irene.

"You're such a great friend Jay. I love you."

I could feel myself blushing. I wasn't sure whether she really meant it or she'd had a few drinks and wasn't quite herself, though I had a feeling it was the latter.

"I'm trying to sleep right now," I texted back.

What a party animal.

"You're my good friend you know."

"You still out there?" I typed, rubbing my eyes.

"Hell yeah I am. This girl's having a damn good time out here. Why aren't you?"

I turned my phone to silent and reached under the bed to put it away in my suitcase. I could still feel the thumping of the bass in my body as I tried to settle into my sleep.

CHAPTER 7

The smell of coffee hit me as I arrived at the dining hall. It was race day and everyone's nerves were up, including my own. It was a longstanding tradition in the NJRA where on race day; we were not supposed to talk about the race prior to it in fear of jinxing the results.

"You missed karaoke last night," Vinnie said as I sat down between him and Julianne, across the table from Andrew. As usual, I avoided eye contact with Andrew. "It was epic."

"Did you sing?" I asked.

"Yup, sang 'Judith' by A Perfect Circle," Vinnie replied.

"Surprised they had that." I took a sip of orange juice.

"You should've seen Mike singing 'Free Bird'," Julianne added, rubbing her eyes.

"Did you three stay pretty late?"

"Nah, called it a night after the Twister game," Vinnie replied, yawning. There were dark circles under his eyes.

"I kind of snuck out in the middle of that. So did Mike," Julianne said. "He said his old body was all partied out."

"Guess Max and Irene are still sleeping," I said.

"Probably. They stayed until the end, after all." Vinnie replied. "I could use another cup of coffee."

"What time did it finish?" I asked.

"The whole thing was officially done at two, in order to comply with the NJRA policy of twelve hours between drinking and flying," Mike replied. "But apparently some people were still hanging out on the runway after that."

"You should've seen what happened in the photo booth," Andrew said, smirking.

"What happened?" I asked, spreading some butter on my pancakes.

"It was steamy hot." He pulled out a strip of photos from his pocket and tossed them on the table. "Found these on the ground near the photo booth after the two of them left."

It was a strip of four photos showing Irene kissing and putting her hands all over a dark-skinned woman.

"Who is she?" I asked.

"Didn't pay attention, but it sure was hot," Andrew added. "Too bad their clothes stayed on."

He seemed genuinely disappointed at that fact.

"Why do you care so much about her personal life?" Julianne cut in.

"Because I never knew she was into Latinas."

It was when he mentioned Latinas that I figured out Irene had been making out with Sara Reyes, a racer from SoCal Jet Racing League. She was the only Latina in the nationals. But I didn't say anything. I was just not the type to gossip.

ANDY DAVIDS

That afternoon, Max and I were both scheduled to have a meet-and-greet with the fans before the race. I walked to the meet-and-greet tents near the grandstands, which were starting to fill up. I looked for one with a table that had a piece of paper with my name on it. Several radio stations also had tents set up and there was a face-painting station, where a child was getting her face painted like a tiger. A lineup of fans, some holding Team Jay signs, weaved their way around the tents. "Jay Smith, Jay Smith, Jay Smith," they chanted as I walked up behind the table and picked up one of the Sharpie markers that had been left for us. The tent beside mine must've been for Max, but it was empty.

"Hey Jay, can you sign this?" a teenage fan with purple streaks in her hair said, handing me a printout of the tutu plane. "You going to rock the tutu plane this afternoon?"

"Nah, that was just Andrew being a dick," I grumbled, signing the photo while trying not to look at it. I didn't like the thought of that being her souvenir, but it was what she wanted and she was my fan.

I signed several posters, magazines, and some of the Team Jay signs the fans had made as well as more printouts of the tutu plane. My hand started to ache like I was writing an in-class essay, with fan after fan handing me items to sign. There were even some children who had brought hand-drawn pictures of me and my plane, their parents smiling behind them.

About an hour into the signing, Max finally arrived at the meet-and-greet tents. I was surprised that none of my fans had asked me where he was. He looked like he had cleaned up well from the night before, though I could see the dark circles around his eyes. He stood behind the table next to mine. Some of the fans in my line moved over to form a new line in front of Max to my disappointment. I guess some of them didn't want to pick a favourite, but were just excited to meet any racer.

"Jay, it's you!" a girl who looked about eighteen years old shouted as she approached the table. She turned her back toward me and pulled down the waistband of her pants, revealing her black lacy panties. *I don't like where this is going at all.*

"Remember me?" she said. "I want you to sign my butt!"

I rolled my eyes at that request, trying to hide my awkwardness. She must have been Leanna from the chat room, who'd asked if I would sign her butt.

"What're you waiting for?" She picked up the marker and shoved it into my hand. "Don't you care about your fans?"

I felt sick to my stomach just thinking about it, even though I did care about my fans. My mind was racing, trying to come up with a reason to refuse. It was then I remembered that a year ago, the NJRA had introduced a policy against signing any part of a person's body due to concerns around sexual harassment. *Looks like I dodged that bullet.*

"I'm not allowed to sign anyone's body; it's the rules," I explained to her. "I'd be happy to sign your ticket or your program if you'd like."

She stomped her foot on the ground before pulling her pants back up and walking away from the table. I swear I had heard Max laughing at my predicament from the table over.

Max's lineup was soon longer than mine. It was obvious who the more popular racer was. I had finished signing and decided I needed a break from the fans. I needed to shake off that disgusted feeling after that butt-signing request.

We met up with Irene, Andrew, Vinnie, and Julianne who weren't signing autographs. Instead, they were just hanging out and chatting near the entrance to the racers' building.

"See that guy over there?" Irene said, pointing to a table to the far right of the one I was signing autographs at. A somewhat tall guy wearing a purple flight jacket was signing there. "That's New York Larry. Watch out for him."

"Is he fast?" I asked.

"Hell yeah. His turn game is spot on, too."

"You can take me out of the East Coast, but you can't take the East Coast out of me," Andrew interrupted.

"Really now, Andrew?" Vinnie added.

"He *almost* took fourth place from me at the East Coast Qualifier," Andrew bragged.

Two hours later, it was race time. All twenty planes were lined up wingtip to wingtip behind a yellow line painted on the tarmac. Their fuselages created a rainbow of colours.

"See you at the finish line," Vinnie said, zipping up his flight jacket. He shook my hand before making his way over to his #37.

"Let's see what you're made of," Andrew shouted, striding toward his plane.

THE JET RACER

I was met with the flashes of several photographers' cameras as I walked down the line, hiding my nerves behind a slight smile. Members of the pit crew had just finished cleaning my #80. A decal of the NJRA logo with the word "Nationals" below it had been added to the tailfin. It made me feel so special, even though all of the other planes had one on their tailfins too.

My eyes widened as I saw Mike walking toward me from the pit area.

"Remember, when you make a turn, keep your movements as minimal as possible, so you don't create too much drag. Other than that, all the best," he said, patting me on the back. He turned around and returned to the pit area.

A couple members of the pit crew moved from plane to plane, handing each of us a map of the race course. I unfolded mine and had a glance through the course, a figure-8 that led us around an oblong lake. Printed on the corner of the map was a set of instructions:

'This course contains 5 electronic checkpoints, marked on the map with a red circle. They register your time via transponder when flown over. You must fly over all checkpoints on all 5 laps in order to avoid disqualification. An electronic map of the course has been downloaded to your navigation system for your reference.'

I looked over the checkpoints placed at different parts of the course. The first checkpoint was the starting line. The second checkpoint was right over the lower right edge of the lake. The third, over the water where the upper and lower parts of the figure-8 met, would be flown over twice on each lap. The fourth one was on the far upper edge of the lake, opposite the first checkpoint at the starting line. We'd have to make a wide pylon turn to reach it. And the fifth was on the edge of the lake opposite the second one.

The grandstands that ran along the side of the starting line were full of excited fans. The announcer's voice boomed over their shouts and cheers. "Ladies and gentlemen! Good afternoon. My name is Jack Davids and I'll be your announcer. On behalf of the NJRA, I'd like to welcome you all to round one of the NJRA nationals."

The crowd did the wave. I looked up at the giant screen across from the grandstands. The camera panned the line of racers standing next to their planes.

Rock guitar riffs played on the sound system as Jack began to announce the names of the racers. "On the far end of the runway with the purple plane with the white lightning bolts, #19 Larry Lorenzi!"

The crowd roared in unison.

"Next up in the forest green #55, Joe Stevenson!" The crowd chanted and applauded between the announcements.

"Flying the blue #37, a rookie pilot this year, Vinnie Giaconia! In the red and gold #52 with the dragons, Irene Chan! In the yellow #10 with the orange flames, we have another rookie, Julianne Madison!"

The crowd screamed louder for Vinnie than for Irene.

"Flying the black #67, the man behind the height, Max Erikson!"

The crowd roared and stomped their feet louder than it did for all of the previous names. I could see on the screen that a bunch of "Team Max" and "Go Erikson 67" signs popped up from the stands and waved in the air. There was even a sign that said "Six Foot Six Will Finish Quick" with "#TeamMax" under it in smaller black letters.

I wasn't going to let it get to me. Even with all the support for Max pouring out of the grandstands, I heard a section of fans on the far left side chanting "Team Jay! Team Jay! Team Jay!"

Several names had passed, the crowd cheering every time the announcer paused. Some of the racers got louder cheers than others, but none as loud as Max's.

"Flying the black and grey striped #80, the youngest contender this year at only twenty-one years old, Jay Smith!"

I was the last one in line. I forced myself to smile, holding back any signs of nervousness, as the camera panned across to me, showing me next to my plane on the screen. Several signs reading "Team Jay," "Go Smith 80," and "We Love Number 8-0" flipped up and waved back and forth in the stands. I could not tell if the crowd had cheered louder for me than they did for Max, but it was close.

"Ladies and gentlemen, let us rise and remove our hats for the singing of the national anthem. Please welcome the Valley Children's Choir."

A choir of thirty or so children wearing red, white, and blue shirts assembled themselves by shirt colour in the middle of the runway facing the grandstands. They began singing, led by their conductor. The screen showed them up close and I was impressed by how coordinated those thirty kids were. They certainly sounded a lot better than the anthem singer at the qualifier.

The choir was led off the runway by their conductor. I climbed into the cockpit of #80 and shut the canopy. One at a time, down the line, the racers each said their names followed by their numbers into their radio.

"Jet Racer Eight Zero, avionics on," I said into my headset.

"Tower to Jet Racers, copy that," said the voice from the control tower. "Jet Racers, start your engines."

My heart was pounding. I was already drenched in sweat under my flight jacket as I placed my feet on the rudder pedals and laid my hands onto the controls.

The control tower began counting down. "Three... two... one..."

I released the brakes and worked the throttle forward as the starting horn blasted. I picked up speed quickly as I raced down the runway. I brought the nose upwards and began my ascent as I reached the end of it.

Andrew's voice came over the radio. "Jet Racer Three Three to Tower, I have an engine failure, aborting takeoff sequence."

I could hear the panic in his voice.

"Tower copy."

I looked down at the runway behind me. The solid white loaner plane Andrew was in skidded to a stop. A cloud of smoke billowed from the engine.

"Jet Racer Eight Zero to Tower, switching to racers' channel. We will be monitoring," I said, then switched the channel on the radio.

I heard Irene's voice. "Oh my God, is he alright?"

"How did that happen?" Vinnie asked.

I heard the rumble of all the engines around me as we reached racing altitude, ten thousand feet. I flipped the switch to turn on my smoke system. My GPS beeped once to indicate the start of the first lap of five. On my left, I saw a purple plane racing up behind. It had to be Larry Lorenzi, also known as New York Larry. His was the only purple plane in the race. A quick glance at the navigation window revealed seven planes ahead of me.

The GPS beeped as I flew over the second checkpoint. I pushed the throttle further forward to gain a bit more speed. I quickly overtook Larry. He would have a bit of catching up to do.

I soon caught up to the plane directly ahead of me; it was #78, Justin Gordon from Portland. I didn't like that guy one bit. I backed down on the throttle, preparing for the banked turn that led to the wide pylon turn. I pushed the control stick to the left and stomped down on the rudder pedal. I could feel my body moving with the forces.

Justin was only a few feet in front of me. I managed to close the gap on him despite slowing down for that turn. *Minimal movements, minimal movements,* I thought. I went in for the wide pylon turn that comprised the smaller, upper part of the figure-8. I took extra care to minimize my movements with the control stick as I flew over the third and fourth checkpoints.

There were two planes in my view as I approached the fifth checkpoint. One was solid grey and the other red. I didn't need to see the numbers on the tailfins to know that the red one was definitely Irene. After all, she was the only one with a red plane in the race.

I took a quick look at the navigation window and saw a plane quickly narrowing the gap behind me. I attempted to get ahead of both of them by pitching almost ninety degrees to the horizon and threading the needle between them, but I only managed to pass the grey one. Irene seemed to have better reaction than me and sped ahead. My GPS beeped as I flew over the fifth checkpoint.

The GPS beeped twice as I reached the starting line checkpoint to mark the start of my second lap. I took a quick look at the leaderboard display in the lower left corner of the heads-up display. The top five from first to fifth were #55 Joe Stevenson, #12 Russ Baird, #67 Max Erikson, #37 Vinnie Giaconia, and #52 Irene Chan.

Shortly after crossing the second checkpoint on the second lap, I quickly closed in on Irene. Her distinct gold ailerons flashed in my peripheral vison as I managed to pass her right as my GPS beeped for the third checkpoint. I turned my head towards her plane and made a friendly nod, although I didn't really care whether she noticed or not. As I watched my name replace hers on the leaderboard, I felt a small warm glow of pride inside me.

As my GPS beeped to indicate the forth checkpoint, Max's name swapped places with Russ's, moving him up to second. I made the pylon turn around the upper part of the figure-8 course.

The solid blue of Vinnie's fuselage slowly came into

view as I approached the fifth checkpoint. Soon we were flying right next to each other. I could see his face through the clear acrylic of the canopy. Both of our GPSs must've beeped at the same time on that checkpoint.

"Go for it, Jay," I heard his voice through the radio. He made a gesture for me to go ahead of him. I looked at him with bewilderment.

Is he really letting me go ahead?

He gestured again. I managed to stop myself from actually asking the question out loud. I had a feeling that if I tried to carry on a conversation with him, he would just speed ahead of me. I wondered if he was setting me up that way, just so he could fly far ahead of me.

I gave him a friendly wave before slamming the throttle forward and shooting right across the starting line checkpoint. The GPS beeped three times to indicate the third lap. There were no planes immediately in view as I flew over the second checkpoint. I flew right through the third checkpoint without too much thought, minding my speed and movements on the turns as Mike had advised.

I switched my radio from the racers' to the commentator's channel for a moment.

"Smith's closing in quickly on Baird, not far off from the fourth checkpoint," the announcer said. "It's all up to how he takes that pylon turn."

I switched back to the racers' channel. I was determined to make it through that upcoming turn without losing too much speed so I could catch up to Russ. I went in for the turn, minding my movements with the control stick and flying over the fourth checkpoint as I completed the turn.

A solid white plane came into view ahead of me. Slamming the throttle forward for a burst of speed, I shot right over the fifth checkpoint, getting ahead of Russ. The black number 12 on the tailfin flashed in my peripheral vision. Another glow of pride filled me as I glanced at the leaderboard and saw my name swap places with his in the yellow rectangle, bringing me up to third place. At the same time, Max's name had swapped with Joe's, putting him in first place.

My GPS beeped four times as I flew over the first checkpoint again, marking the fourth lap. Joe was still far enough away that I couldn't see him as I flew over the second checkpoint. I switched my radio to the commentator's channel again as I crossed the third checkpoint.

"Erikson's leading the way towards the finish line after getting ahead of Stevenson effortlessly. He's blazing across the sky, passing the fourth checkpoint with a real smooth pylon turn!"

My grip tightened on the control stick and throttle.

"Now Smith's closing the gap on Stevenson as he goes in for that pylon turn! It's all down to that turn for him now! Will he make it through smoothly like Erikson did?"

I approached the pylon turn and forced my mind to go blank. I took a few deep breaths and let my muscle memory take me through. My GPS beeped for the fourth checkpoint.

Smooth, just like Erikson.

"What a splendid pylon turn from Smith, ladies and gentlemen! And now he's going balls to the wall, closing in on

Stevenson as he heads toward the fifth checkpoint!"

Over the radio, I could hear the muffled sound of the crowd in the background. "Go Jay, go Jay, go Jay!" they chanted. My heart pounded as I heard "Go Max!" mixed in.

I switched my radio back to the racers' channel.

"You can do it, Jay!"

I was pretty sure it was Vinnie's voice, though I didn't have time to think about it.

"I believe in you!" I recognized that voice as Julianne's.

I glanced at the leaderboard display. Vinnie was now in fourth place with Julianne behind him. My GPS beeped five times as I crossed the first checkpoint for the fifth and final lap of the race.

Another glance at the navigation screen revealed that someone was catching up behind me. I had a good feeling it was Russ. I was soon on Joe Stevenson's tail. I paid extra attention to controlling my speed so I wouldn't be slowed down by the turn leading to the second checkpoint. I managed to pass Joe without too much effort as I crossed the checkpoint. The warm feeling of pride and excitement was starting to get familiar as I watched my name swap places with his on the leaderboard, putting me right below Max.

You can do it, Jay, you can do it.

I watched on the navigation screen as Max headed for the pylon turn. My hands trembled on the controls as I approached the turn.

I focused all my attention on trying to avoid excessive drag. My GPS beeped for the third checkpoint. I was on Max's tail.

You can do it, Jay, you can do it. Don't think, just fly.

Without hesitation, I slammed the throttle all the way forward, sending my plane soaring past him like an asteroid entering the earth's atmosphere. I continued at full speed, the force of acceleration pushing me back against the seat as I pushed my plane to its limits. Through my headset, the roar of the powerful engine drowned out the thoughts inside my head.

Max had quickly caught back up to me. We flew side by side for a few seconds, and then I pulled ahead. I completed the pylon turn and my GPS beeped for the fourth checkpoint.

The fifth checkpoint inched closer and closer on the navigation screen. I could see Max was closing in quickly. I brought the throttle back up again and waited for the beep. The GPS beeped as I flew over the fifth checkpoint. I prepared for the final banked turn leading back to the starting line.

I was closing in on that final checkpoint. My hands clenched the controls. I watched Vinnie's name move up to third, bringing Russ down to fourth. Then, out of nowhere, Max's plane rushed right past me. I hadn't seen that coming. My stomach sank as our names switched back to their previous places, leaving me to finish in second.

How can it end this way?

"Not so easy, huh, Jay?" Max taunted on the radio.

"Guess we'll see next round," I replied, gritting my teeth.

"Second's not bad," Vinnie said.

Not bad, huh?

"At least you gave it your best," Irene added.

THE JET RACER

I didn't know what to say to Vinnie or Irene. I could not believe what had just happened; I must have slowed down a bit too much on that last banked turn. I was so determined not to lose to Max in the next round.

I switched the radio to the tower communication channel.

"Jet Racer Eight Zero to Tower, preparing for landing," I said into my headset. I flipped the switch to shut off my smoke system. I deployed the landing gear and extended the flaps.

"Jet Racer Eight Zero, you are clear for landing."

The back wheels touched down on the runway, followed by the front wheels. I continued easing off on the throttle as I applied the brakes. The air traffic controller pointed me toward the area in front of the hangars. I taxied over to the spot where I was directed. I took my headset off and opened the canopy, hanging my head in shame. The crowd cheered loudly. I looked up to see both Team Max and Team Jay signs waving in the stands. And just like before the race, the cheering for Max was much louder than it was for me.

CHAPTER 8

"Jay Smith, you had us all on the edge of our seats during that race!" Jack Davids's voice said over the stadium sound system. Just hearing that gave me a slight sense of pride, despite the disappointing results of that race.

As Vinnie's blue #37 landed on the runway moments later, Jack's voice boomed over the sound system again.

"What a surprising performance from Vinnie Giaconia there. What tremendous improvement over what we saw of him at the West Coast Qualifier!"

Vinnie taxied to the area in front of the hangars. He parked his plane next to mine, then opened his canopy and climbed out of the cockpit. A photographer set up a tripod in front of us. Several more set up to our right, surrounding Max's plane.

I smiled and did my best to act excited about the race results while hiding my frustration at having lost that racce to Max.

"Great flying there, Vinnie," I said, shaking his hand.

"I let you pass so you could get past Max and you let this happen?" Vinnie muttered under his breath.

Is he actually mad at me or just saying that?

"He caught up to me," I snapped. "I swear I was just about to cross the finish line."

The sound of shouting came from behind us. It was unmistakably Max's voice. Vinnie and I both turned to look. I watched as Max threw a reporter's microphone on the ground and shoved three cameras away. *Oh my God, what's going on with him?*

"Somebody get security!" another voice shouted. It was Russ Baird. He was running away from Max and his face was all red.

"You're a disease to the NJRA!" Max yelled at Russ, sticking up his middle finger.

I stood there, petrified, my heart pounding and my hands sweaty. The photographers haed started taking down their equipment.

"Man, you alright?" I heard Vinnie's voice as if from a distance.

"Uh, yeah," I replied, stuttering.

"Never mind Max. That was completely uncalled for."

"Yeah, no doubt," I sighed.

"Let's go," he said, patting me on the back.

I followed Vinnie back to the racers' building. The refreshing feeling of the air conditioning hit me in the face the moment I stepped indoors.

"I took your advice, Jay," Vinnie said, smiling. "Remember what you said about listening to the plane and getting the feel of it?"

"You did great," I replied.

Joe Stevenson walked toward us. He was carrying two bowls, one full of popcorn and the other filled to the brim with cashews and almonds. "Would you guys like some popcorn or nuts?" he asked. Suddenly, I was starving. That popcorn looked delicious.

"Sure, thanks, Joe," I said, grabbing a handful of popcorn.

"You killed that pylon turn on the last lap," he said.

"I've been working on it," I replied. "But I really wasn't expecting you-know-who to sneak up on me like that," I explained, trying not to show my disappointment. "Thought I was far enough ahead.

"You're the guy from Nevada, right?" Vinnie asked, taking a handful of cashews and almonds. "Saw you at the qualifier but didn't get a chance to talk to you."

I remembered Joe from the qualifier, as well as an interview in *Modern Pilot* about his experiences of being an African American pilot in the NJRA.

"Yep, Desert Jet Racing League in Nevada," Joe replied.

"Ah, near Las Vegas?"

"Bit of a ways from there."

"You ever have issues with dust storms?" Vinnie asked.

"It can be pretty bad at times," Joe said. "In that case they'll issue a weather notice."

"Must be a challenge to maintain your plane in those conditions," Vinnie said.

"Our league caretaker always complains about having to clean all the sand off the planes after a storm," Joe said.

"Kind of jealous of your weather in Washington State."

"I take it you like rain?" I asked.

"Of course," he replied. "We only get it once in a blue moon."

"The Pacific Northwest is actually a rainforest," Vinnie added. "Hence all the rain we get."

"Where are you off to now?" Joe asked.

"Going to the sleeping quarters to change, check my emails, and whatnot," I replied. "What about you?"

"Just on my way to the leisure room to shoot some pool. Saw you two and thought I'd say hi."

"I'll catch you later," Vinnie said. "Going to take a shower."

Joe continued down the hallway toward the leisure room. Vinnie and I walked in the opposite direction to the men's sleeping quarters. We ran into Mike along the way. His clothes were covered in dust and grease.

"You got this, Jay," he said, giving me a high five.

"I'm going to have to reconsider how I fly if I want to finish first," I grumbled.

"You gave it your best. That's what matters."

"Yeah, I know, but I still feel bad about how the race ended."

"This ain't the time to be feeling sorry for yourself," Mike replied.

I nodded.

"You really want to pay more attention to that pylon turn," he said. "Remember to make sure you start your roll early on. You don't want to lose speed."

"I'll keep that in mind." *Start roll early on, start roll early on.* "By the way, I have my logs from yesterday."

As Mike waited in the hall, I grabbed my logbook from my suitcase, took out the previous day's log, and handed it to Mike.

"Thanks," he said, walking down the hallway.

I took my flight jacket off, changed into a clean T-shirt, and sat down on my bed. I'd planned to check my email, but I was too worn out from the race. I flipped open the Bruce Dickinson book to where I had last left off. I tried to focus on the words, but the thoughts of the race earlier that day kept creeping into my head.

Out the corner of my eye, I caught a glimpse of Julianne in the hallway. She was probably going back to the women's sleeping quarters. Her hair was tied back in a messy bun and her clothes were covered in sweat and dust. She was definitely not as glamorous as she was in that magazine photo Max had been eyeing a couple nights before. I almost wanted to go outside to say hi to her, but at the same time, I didn't feel like getting out of my bed. I was just too upset with that race.

I went back to reading. I was almost three-quarters of the way into the book. I'd never given much thought to Bruce Dickinson before Max lent me this book. I knew he was a talented musician, but now I was discovering that he was a fascinating character with a vast variety of knowledge, a Renaissance man, as my old English teacher would have called him.

The thought of Max made me shut the book and toss it

onto the floor. An image of him passing me just before the finish line rushed into my head. I took out my laptop and decided to just lay back and listen to music instead.

My eyes darted toward the doorway as I heard the sound of footsteps. It was Russ. He dragged himself to the bed across from mine, his head down. He let out a sigh as he sat down on the bed and kicked his boots off.

"You alright?" I asked.

"I wouldn't be looking like this if I was," he said, wiping the sweat off his forehead with his sleeve.

"What happened out there?"

He got up off his own bed and sat down on the edge of Vinnie's.

"It's all Max's fault."

I nodded. *At least someone else shares my feelings about Max.*

"You see, when he was trying to pass me in the second lap," he continued, "he came a bit too close for comfort. I swear he was going to hit me."

"Wow."

"He made sure his smoke system sprayed smoke right into me," Russ explained. "My canopy was covered with smoke oil, although the wind quickly took care of that."

"That's awful." I might have lost first place to Max by a couple of seconds, but at least he hadn't tried to blind me.

"So when we landed, I went over to tell him off. I was going to say 'you're the one who sprayed me with smoke oil,' but I know I'd only be adding fuel to the fire. He got pissed and grabbed me pretty hard."

"Were you hurt?" I asked.

"Not really," he said, pointing at the bruises on his arms. "He let me go and walked away like he was trying to avoid the rest of the cameras after throwing the reporter's mic on the ground earlier."

Russ paused and rubbed his arm. "Guess he'd realized what he did and regretted it."

"At least you're okay. I know he can get pretty angry, but I've never seen him get physical with anyone."

"The competition brings out the worst in people," he explained. "What can I say?"

I couldn't remember any time where I'd gotten so mad at another racer that I wanted to beat them to the ground. But it was the nationals, after all. I could only imagine what kinds of things happen in the World Series.

"I guess you probably need some time to yourself after that." *I sure would.*

"I'll be okay, but let's talk about something else. Are you and Vinnie good friends?"

"Guess you could say that. We do have quite a bit in common."

"That guy's really something. I mean, for someone who's just out of training camp."

"Definitely, if he keeps it up, it's easy to see who this year's rookie of the year will be," I replied.

"Between him, Ray, and Julianne, I'd pick Julianne. I mean, just look at her!"

I sighed. "Don't you think skill matters more than looks when it comes to choosing the rookie of the year?"

"Why do you think I wasn't rookie of the year four years ago when I started? I was almost two hundred pounds back then. Nobody wants to vote for an overweight, out-of-shape pilot."

"I guess I'm not bad looking, but I didn't make the list last year." *I guess nobody likes short guys who look almost five years younger than they are.*

"It took a lot to keep all those nosy people off my back. They were dying to know how I lost all that weight in the off-season." he chuckled. "A good trainer and cutting down on carbs was all it took."

When Vinnie entered the sleeping quarters, Russ stood up and walked back over to his own bed. Vinnie pulled his backpack out from under his bed and took out his laptop as well as *Advanced Jet Racing Strategies*.

"Thanks for lending me this," he said, handing the book to me. "It was a great read."

"Glad to hear," I said as I put the book away in my suitcase.

"Would you mind if I borrow that Bruce Dickinson book for a bit?" Vinnie asked.

"It's not mine, though," I answered. "Might be better to ask Max."

Then again, maybe asking Max wasn't a good idea.

"Just for a couple days? I promise I'll give it back."

"Alright, but be careful with it," I replied. "He didn't say I could lend it to anyone else."

I just didn't want to think about Max anymore, and if I let Vinnie borrow the book, it would be out of my hands for a couple days. Out of sight, out of mind.

"Don't worry, I won't let him see me reading it." He picked the book up off the floor, glancing toward the doorway to make sure Max wasn't anywhere nearby. He flipped it open and began reading, already absorbed into it from the start.

Russ was busy on his laptop, so I checked my text messages. There was one from my adoptive dad.

"Great race Jay!"

"Thanks," I texted back.

He answered right away. "Mom and I are proud of you. Now let's see you on that podium!"

"Wasn't expecting Max to sneak up on me like that."

"Life's full of twists and turns Jay. Never know what's going to happen." He sure was trying to cheer me up about ending the first round of the nationals in second place.

"Sure heard that a million times." I definitely had heard that a million times, in some form or another.

"How's the stadium? Nice?"

"Much better than Reno. Beds are comfy, food's pretty good, can't believe there's even a spa here," I explained.

"No more soggy waffles?"

"Don't remind me."

"A hungry pilot isn't a happy one."

"Wasn't the stadium's fault, caterer slacked off." *And they sure slacked off.*

"Any plans for the rest of the day?"

"Dinner soon, then relax in the hot tub."

"There's a hot tub at the stadium?"

"Yes and the spa does facials and whatnot."

"Sounds fancy. What do you think of Salt Lake Valley?"

"It's nice I guess."

"They sure picked a great location. Enjoy your dinner."

I was just about to get up when he sent one more message. "By the way, we're cleaning the attic and found three boxes of your old stuff. You might want to come home and sort through them after the nationals. Otherwise we'll just donate it all."

I put my phone back in my pocket without bothering to reply. I had no idea what kind of stuff was in those boxes. Probably just old school supplies. I couldn't care less if they donated those. I stood up from my bed.

"Heading to dinner?" Russ asked, looking up from his laptop screen.

"Yep."

"I'll be there in a bit. Chatting with my wife right now and she's not exactly happy."

"How about you, Vinnie?"

"Yeah, just let me finish dealing with these last few emails."

I made my way to the dining hall. Irene and Julianne were standing at the doors, waiting for them to open. The smell of food wafted out, but I couldn't tell what exactly it was.

Julianne was wearing sandals, and I couldn't help but notice that her toenails were painted phoenix orange. It matched her nail polish.

"I like your toe polish," I said hesitantly.

"Just got a pedicure at the spa. I usually don't do my toes, but since it's free, I was like what the heck."

"Looks nice."

I had always wondered what it was like to get a pedicure, or a manicure, at a spa. One time, when I was younger, my adoptive mom said she was going to the salon for a manicure. I said, "I want a manicure too." I'd never forget the look of disgust on her face. "Only girls get them," she'd snapped.

"Speaking of the spa, I'm going to the hot tub after dinner. Either of you want to come along?" I asked.

"Sure, I've got nothing else to do," Irene replied.

"I'll have to see," Julianne said. "Got to make an important phone call to one of my sponsors."

"Something smells yummy," Irene said, looking through the window of the dining hall doors. "These NJRA events are always so fancy."

"No doubt," I added.

"That was some pretty wicked flying," Irene said. "You were so close to first place."

"Ah, Max," I glanced around me, making sure he wasn't in the vicinity.

"You could've kicked his ass there." I heard a voice with a heavy New York accent behind me. It was Larry.

I didn't bother to respond to him, because I knew exactly why Max had managed to catch up to me right before the final checkpoint.

The doors to the dining hall opened. I followed Irene and Julianne and took a seat at the same table as them. An ice sculpture of an NJRA jet, surrounded by plates of sliced up fruit served as a centrepiece for the buffet table.

I made my way up to the food line. Julianne was taking pictures of the buffet table as well as the ice sculpture, which was already dripping into the glass tray under it.

"I don't understand the point of these things," I said, pointing to the ice sculpture.

"What do you mean? I like it," Julianne responded. "It just makes everything seem so much fancier."

Fancier was definitely the right word. They didn't have ice sculptures at Reno.

"They want to show us how well they're treating us, don't they?" Irene added.

"They look nice, but they don't last." After all, it would be nothing more than an unrecognizable chunk of ice floating in a puddle by the end of the night.

Despite my opinion about ice sculptures, I took a moment to admire this one. An artist would have spent hours carving it before the big event, only for it to melt away and get poured down the drain at the end of it all. I snapped a few photos on my phone and texted them to Dad. There wasn't any particular racer's number carved into it, but everything, right down to the shape of the canopy and the bolts on the wings, was carefully carved with such intricate detail that grew more indistinct with each drip of water into the puddle below.

I carried my loaded plate back to our table. Max arrived, strutting right past us as he headed for the buffet.

"Vinnie's sitting there," I said as Max put his plate on

the table and tried to take the seat to my left. He picked up his plate, gave me and Irene a stare, and then walked away without a word.

I was so stuffed from all that food, I had to skip dessert. I stopped at the buffet table on my way out to admire the ice sculpture one last time. The ailerons on the wings had melted into a blur, and the entire sculpture was slowly disintegrating, drop by drop, into the clear glass tray below.

When I got back to the men's sleeping quarters, I pulled my suitcase out from under my bed and unzipped it. I riffled through all my clothes to find my swimsuit. I had also brought along a tank top to wear with it, as going topless just never felt right to me.

I arrived at the spa, which was right across from the leisure room. Looking at the plain metal door with a plastic sign on it that said "SPA" in black letters, I wasn't sure what to expect. I was greeted by the calm scent of lavender oil as I walked into the dimmed room. Soft classical music was playing from the speakers. The air was humid, not unlike at an indoor pool, but without the strong smell of chlorine. There were candles in glass holders all over the place. As I looked a little closer, I could tell they were electronic from the way they flickered, which I imagined was for safety reasons.

"Welcome," a woman with curly blonde hair sitting at a desk said in a soft, airy voice. "What can we do for you today?"

"I'd like to use the hot tub."

"Just follow the hallway to the end and you'll see the change rooms on each side. When you're ready, the hot tub is just through the glass door at the end."

She handed me a towel.

I followed the hallway until I reached the glass door. On each side of the hallway was a door, both simply marked "Change Room." I guessed neither one was the men's or the women's, as there were no signs indicating so. I opened the one on the right and was relieved to see that it was for only one person at a time as I wouldn't have to share a change room with anyone else. All those naked bodies in public change rooms made for some pretty uncomfortable situations. I locked the door behind me and got changed into my swimsuit.

As I walked into the hot tub room, I was struck by how big the hot tub was. It was the size of the toddler pool at a community centre. On the walls all around it, shelves held more electric candles. Vinnie and Irene were already there, sitting at the far end. I climbed into the hot tub with a light splash and waded over to them. I sat down next to Vinnie.

"Ohhhh, this is so relaxing," I said, dipping my head and face in the water for a second. I sat back up and brushed my hair out of my face.

"I know, right?" Vinnie replied. "Got all your official stuff done, Jay?"

"Didn't have much of that, just my flight logs."

"Never knew you had a tattoo," Vinnie said, looking at the faded black outline of a sailboat about the size of a business card a few inches above my right elbow. I was surprised he had never noticed it before. I hoped he wasn't trying to tell me how impressive it was as it looked pretty much like a four-year-old's drawing.

"Had it since I was sixteen."

"Is there, like, a story behind it?" he asked. "You don't have to tell me if you don't want to."

"It's a sailboat on the ocean," I said. More like a half-faded sailboat with a portion of its sail missing. "I guess it means that I'll always be going to new places."

"That sounds like me. I'm always going new places too."

"I didn't really think about any meaning at the time," I explained. "A few friends and I decided not to go to Spanish class one day, so we went to hang out at Roman's Pizza. We were chatting and eating, and one of them asked if I wanted a tattoo. I thought it sounded like a cool idea, so we went into the bathroom, where he did it with a safety pin and India ink over the baby-changing table."

Vinnie cringed as I told the story. I couldn't blame him, thinking back to how stupid an idea that was.

"It was a miracle it didn't get infected or anything, though it probably helped that he heated the safety pin with a lighter beforehand. But it didn't occur to me at the time what kind of nasty germs were on the changing table."

"Do you ever want to get it redone, like by a professional?" Vinnie asked.

"I've thought about getting it covered up. But I can't decide what I want to cover it with."

"You could always get a naked busty girl like Max's," he said, smirking.

"Vinnie!" I splashed water at him.

"I got one too," Irene said, standing up in the hot tub.

"A naked girl?" Vinnie asked.

I can imagine Irene with that.

"A stick and poke," she said, pointing at her right hip. "Yeah, it's a doughnut with a bite taken out of it."

"Not bad," I replied. At least hers wasn't all faded, and I could tell immediately what it was.

"Got it in university before I quit. Cliché, I know."

"I'm sure we can figure out the rest." Vinnie giggled under his breath.

Irene sat down.

"Hey, have either of you heard anything about Andrew?" she asked. "Just wondered where he's been after what happened at the start of the race."

"Pretty sure I saw him waiting in the buffet line earlier, but that's about it," Vinnie replied. "I can only imagine how upset Mike must be now at all the damage he's done."

"Yeah, since he's now got two planes to fix," Irene said.

"Just Andrew's personal one," I said. "Mike won't be fixing the loaner since it's not league property."

"Poor guy needs to catch a break soon," Vinnie added.

"I imagine Andrew's paycheque's going to take a big dent," Irene said. "Although I guess today's engine failure wasn't really his fault."

"But that pancake landing was definitely his fault," I added.

"Maybe whoever inspected his loaner plane missed something?" Vinnie asked.

"Could very well be," I said.

"What do you think of the spa?" Irene asked.

"It's really nice. I like that the hot tub doesn't have that swimming pool smell. All those chemicals make my skin itchy."

"They're probably using ozone," Vinnie said. "It's better for people with sensitive skin."

"Anyway, I just remembered that I still haven't checked my emails, so I should go do that before it gets too late."

"You better go do that then," Irene replied. "I'll see you tomorrow."

Chapter 9

Larry's voice broke into my nightmare as I woke up that morning. "Whoever was sleep-talking last night, it sure sounded like you were having a good time," he said, yawning.

"Well, I couldn't sleep because of you, asshole," Max responded, getting out of his bed.

As they continued arguing, I quickly got dressed and went to the bathroom to brush my teeth. I walked down to the dining hall, trying to shake off the lingering feeling of that nightmare. Vinnie, Irene, and Julianne were sitting at a table together. I sat down next to Vinnie.

"Everything okay, Jay?" Vinnie asked. "You look a bit shaky."

"It's probably just pre-race nervousness," I said.

"I'm going out for a jog around the stadium. You guys want to come?" Irene asked. "It'll help with the nerves."

"Yeah, why not?" Vinnie glanced at his watch for a second. "We've got plenty of time and I'm a little nervous too now that I think about it."

"For sure," I replied, scooping a spoonful of cereal

from my bowl.

"I'll come too," Julianne added. "Might as well do something with all the energy from that coffee."

We returned to the sleeping quarters to change into exercise attire before following Irene out of the racers' building.

"Did all of you sleep well last night?" Irene asked.

"Not exactly. Had a pretty intense nightmare, only to be woken up by Max and Larry yelling at each other," I replied.

"Guess I missed the yelling," Vinnie said. "Both of them were still sleeping when I got up."

"I could hear it from the women's sleeping quarters, but I couldn't tell what they were shouting about," Irene said.

"Anyways, I dreamed that I saw my adoptive mom in the crowd," I explained. "She ran all the way down to the pit area where the pit crew was just starting to get the planes ready. She kept screaming at me in front of everyone, telling me what a waste of my life jet racing was and that I should just give up flying and go finish high school instead; all while everyone else just stood there staring at me."

"That doesn't sound good," Vinnie replied. "At least it was just a dream, and besides, you don't see her anymore."

"So, anyone know what happened to Andrew?" Julianne asked. "I haven't seen him around since last night."

"He wasn't in the men's sleeping quarters this morning either," Vinnie responded. "Probably took a cab into town."

I hadn't paid much attention to Andrew, so I'd no idea that he hadn't been in the men's sleeping quarters. Then again, I didn't think I had any reason to be paying attention to who was and wasn't there in the morning.

We began jogging past the hangars toward the runway. There was no one else outside except for the four of us. The only sounds we could hear were the rhythmic thumping of our footsteps and the faint buzzing of power tools as the pit crew worked on the planes. I'd never really been into jogging, but I noticed my nervousness slowly melting away with every step.

"Speak of the devil," Irene said, looking toward the hangars. I turned my head in that direction. Andrew was leaving the hangars and heading toward the racers' building. He didn't seem to notice us.

"I don't know why, but I have a funny feeling," Julianne commented.

"What do you mean?" Vinnie asked.

"Like when you feel something's not right but you can't put your finger on what it is," she replied.

"You're probably just nervous," Vinnie said. "I mean, we're both rookies and we're at the nationals. It's a big deal."

"Yeah, the whole country's eyes are on us," Julianne said.

"Sometimes when I get nervous, I feel like everyone's up to something," Vinnie added.

"But I've been having a bad feeling ever since I arrived here," Julianne explained.

"You'll be fine," I said. "Don't think about it too much."

From inside the hangar, I could see all nineteen jets lined up in a row behind the starting line on the runway. *It just didn't look right without Andrew's plane.* Members of the pit crew were finishing up fueling the last couple of them. My #80 was the eighth one on the line.

"See you in the sky," Vinnie said. He knelt down to pick up his flight jacket off the ground. As he stood back up, he stepped on one of his untied bootlaces, causing him to fall forward and bump into Max, who dropped his headset. It landed on the concrete with a clatter.

"Hey, watch it there," Max snapped. "You trying to get fresh with me now?"

Vinnie scrambled out of Max's way, then bent over to tie his bootlace.

"See you at the finish line," Max spat out. He turned around and left the hangar, walking out to the runway, where he was greeted by several TV cameras. I followed him out to the starting line. I could see that he was facing the cameras with a huge smile on his face.

The announcer's voice on the PA system boomed over the noise of the crowd. "Welcome to round two of the NJRA Nationals. I'm your host, Jack Davids, and today we are getting ready for another adrenaline-fuelled afternoon of racing here in the sunny Utah Valley! We saw a pretty tight finish from Max Erikson yesterday, but it looks like Jay Smith's got a chance too!"

The crowd erupted into cheering as Jack said both of our names.

"Folks, the planes have been oiled and fuelled, the racers are ready to go, but who will cross the finish line first this time? We'll be finding out real soon!"

I looked toward the stands, trying to count whether there were more Team Jay or Team Max signs. There appeared to be an equal number of both. There were even a couple Team Vinnie signs among them. I guess Vinnie was gaining a bit of a fan base himself.

Julianne walked past me on the way to her plane, which was to the left of mine. Her uneasiness was clear in her face.

"You'll be fine, Juli," I said, patting her on the back. I wondered what was wrong. She sure hadn't seemed this nervous the previous day.

"Ladies and gentlemen, please remove your hats and rise," Jack Davids announced. "Now let us welcome Air Force veteran Captain Chris Fernandez and join him in the singing of the national anthem."

An older man in a US Air Force uniform made his way onto the runway with a microphone in his hand. An array of medals and ribbons hung from the left side of his jacket. Captain Fernandez belted out the anthem and the crowd joined him.

As I climbed into the cockpit of #80 after the anthem, I could see all the cameras flashing amid the signs in the stands. The mumbled shouting of "Team Jay, Team Jay, Team Jay!" along with the likes of "Go, Erikson!" faded as I shut the canopy, closing me off from the outside world.

"Jet Racer Eight Zero, avionics on." As the rest of the racers down the line gave their numbers, it felt a bit odd not hearing Andrew's voice among them.

"Tower to Jet Racers, copy that."

"Racers start your engines," I heard Jack Davids say in adset.

The diagram of the figure-8 course loaded up on my navigation screen. I could feel my heart pounding as the countdown to the starting horn began. As soon as I heard the horn, I released the brakes. I gripped the throttle and control stick as I rushed to the end of the runway for takeoff. I flipped the switch for my smoke system.

I quickly overtook Irene as I felt the afterburner kick in. I swore for a second that I heard my adoptive mom's voice in my head cheering me on, quite unlike how she'd been in the dream that morning. If she wasn't out in the stands somewhere, she would probably be in front of the TV back home with the channel locked on ESPN.

A purple plane rushed ahead of me from my right side. I didn't look at the number on the tailfin as it went in for the upcoming turn. I shifted against the left rudder pedal to begin the first turn, trying to catch up to the plane in front of me. The GPS beeped as I flew over the second checkpoint.

I shot right past the purple plane, passing over the third checkpoint. The white #19 on the tailfin flashed in the corner of my eye. I eased off on the throttle as I set myself up for the upcoming pylon turn.

"Tower to Jet Racer Seven Eight, this is a judges' warning. Our systems indicate that you have missed checkpoint four," I heard through the radio. "Please turn around and fly over it to avoid disqualification."

Did Justin Gordon deliberately try to miss that checkpoint? I took advantage of the opportunity to get ahead of him. My GPS beeped as I flew over the fourth checkpoint, completing the pylon turn. I managed to pass three planes before passing over the fifth checkpoint.

My GPS beeped twice as I flew over the starting line, indicating the start of the second lap. I glanced at the leaderboards at the corner of the screen. Ash Christie was leading the race. I watched Max's name switch places with Joe Stevenson's as I went in for my first turn of that lap, passing over the first checkpoint.

As I approached the pylon turn around the upper edge of the lake, I noticed a dot on the figure-8 diagram inching closer to me by the second. Someone was catching up to me. A red and gold plane, which I immediately recognized as Irene's, sped ahead of me as it started its roll for the turn.

Minimize drag, not too much aileron, nose down, start roll early. I began my roll for the pylon turn earlier than I had on the previous lap. After flying over the forth checkpoint and completing that turn, I was catching up to Irene. I pushed the throttle forward, aiming the nose right at the fifth checkpoint. I sped past Irene as my GPS beeped.

Vinnie's name had just swapped places with Robert Taylor's on the leaderboard, putting him in fifth place behind Joe. Max's name also swapped places with Russ Baird's, only to swap back to the previous order a couple seconds later. My GPS beeped three times as I flew over the starting line, passing another plane without much effort. It was Julianne's yellow and orange #10. I switched my radio to the commentator's channel.

"Here we have Ash Christie, the only pilot from Wyoming this year, maintaining his lead, with Russ Baird not too far behind," Jack Davids was saying. "What's this, folks? Vinnie Giaconia is catching up to Joe Stevenson! Look at those moves! Will he pass Joe as he makes his approach toward the upper edge of the lake for the pylon turn?"

As I flew over the second checkpoint, I switched back to the racers' channel. "Vinnie, you can do it," I said into my headset.

"Fly, Jay, fly," I heard Max's deep voice on the radio. "Fly like the little rookie humper you are."

Vinnie's name switched with Joe's on the leaderboard display, bringing him into fourth place. Julianne's #10 rushed in front of me as I began my roll for the pylon turn. Max's name had just swapped places with Russ's as my GPS beeped for the third checkpoint.

Minimize drag, not too much aileron, nose down. I swung myself around the upper part of the figure-8 course. The centrifugal force of the turn pushed my arms into the armrests as I passed the fourth checkpoint. There were only five planes in front of me on the navigation screen. I slammed the throttle as I exited the turn, feeling the rapid change in acceleration pushing my back against the backrest. The adrenaline rushed through me as I heard the roar of the engine through my headset. I watched my dot inching closer to Joe's on the screen as my GPS beeped for the fifth checkpoint.

I decreased my speed and banked to the left in preparation for the last turn leading back to the starting line. I pushed the throttle forward, sending me straight toward the starting line and passing Joe along the way. My GPS beeped four times, indicating the start of my fourth lap. I felt the familiar swell of pride as I watched my name move up to fifth place, putting me right behind Vinnie on the leaderboard.

"Mayday, mayday, may-."

My heart skipped a beat as I heard Julianne's voice on the radio, her last *"mayday"* cut off by a crackling sound. My GPS beeped as I flew over the second checkpoint.

"Oh my God, Juli, what's wrong?" I shouted frantically into my headset.

"Juli, everything okay there?" I could hear the panic in Max's voice. "Julianne Madison! Can you hear me?"

"Juli, what's wrong?" Irene shouted, her voice trembling. "Answer me!"

There was a blast of static, then silence.

"Eject!" Larry shouted. "Now!"

There was no response from Julianne. Sweat dripped from my hands onto the flight controls as the pounding of my heart shook my entire body. I tried to focus on my breathing, which was fast and heavy.

"Shit," Robert shouted. "That can't be good."

Focus, Jay, focus.

"Juli!" I let out.

My GPS beeped as I passed over the fourth checkpoint before exiting the turn. I switched my radio over to the commentator's channel.

"Mathias Stewart's #26 has crashed into the lake. Looks like he was able to eject in time, but his right wing knocked against Julianne Madison's #10 just as she crossed the third checkpoint."

I looked through the side of my canopy while attempting to maintain my direction toward the fifth checkpoint. A yellow and orange jet was falling toward the lake like a coin tossed into a fountain. I wasn't sure whether I was more concerned about Mathias or Julianne in that moment.

Focus, Jay, focus. I had to be careful to not go off course or I'd have had to turn around. Through the clear acrylic of the canopy, I could just make out Julianne in her orange and yellow flight jacket slumped over the instrument console. The black numbers on the tailfin grew smaller and smaller as the plane lost altitude.

The right wing hit the lake first, tearing off instantly. The fuselage slammed into the water, flipping upside down for a second before shattering into pieces. The normally dark surface of the lake turned solid white upon impact. A thick cloud of white mist was thrown into the air. Julianne's #10 was now a pile of orange and yellow debris floating on the surface of the lake.

I glanced at the navigation screen just as her red dot disappeared like a candle being blown out. The entire scene froze inside my mind for a moment. *Wake up, Jay!* This was not simply a bad dream; the solid flight controls my hands were wrapped around were all too real.

"Juli, Juli!" I shouted into my headset, only to realize I was still on the commentator's channel. I could feel my eyes tearing up.

"Stewart appears to be fully conscious as he parachutes down to safety. There is no sign of Madison, nor do we know if she successfully ejected." Jack Davids's voice seemed to have lost its energy.

I switched my radio back to the racers' channel. I was quickly catching up to Vinnie. I was almost on his tail as my GPS beeped for the fifth checkpoint, snapping me back to reality from the intense flood of emotion. Max's name had moved up to first place on the leaderboard, putting Ash and Russ behind him in second and third.

"Don't you dare be dead!" Max shouted over the radio. I could sense the tears he was holding back in his stutter.

"Sounds like she lost communications after that distress call," Larry said.

"Why the hell didn't she eject?" I blurted out.

"Someone did this!" Max cut in. "You're going to pay for it!"

A cold shiver ran through my body, even though I was sweating under my flight jacket, like the chills I'd had from a bad flu years ago. My stomach felt queasy and my eyes were watering. There was a hot feeling in my throat.

My GPS beeped five times, indicating the start of my fifth and final lap. I tried to ignore the conversation on the radio and focus on racing, but the sight of the crash flooded my mind like a song on repeat.

"She might've fallen out of her seat or something," Irene said.

"Sabotage, I know it!" Max cut in again. "You're going to pay for it! You're going to pay for it!"

Focus, Jay, focus. I could hear my heart pounding inside my head, adding to the noise of the conversation coming through my headset. The image of Julianne's *Sports Illustrated* photoshoot crept into my mind, followed by the memory of the time she, Irene, Vinnie, and I were flying with Andrew when he first arrived at Central City.

The beeping of my GPS as I flew over the first checkpoint snapped me back to reality. I passed Vinnie, but barely saw him. I didn't know if he would have just let me pass him like he did on the previous round, but I wasn't going to take a chance.

Minimize drag, less aileron, nose down. The repetition of these instructions helped me to stay calm and focused. My GPS beeped as I passed the second checkpoint. I'd always been an obsessive person, and repeating things helped me to stay calm in intense situations, giving my mind something to focus on.

I prepared for the upcoming pylon turn, paying extra attention to minimizing aileron usage that time. I could not recall a time when I'd put this much thought into executing a pylon turn. Overthinking kept my mind off the horrible scene I'd just witnessed and kept my emotions in check. But even still, I was too slow on the turn. My GPS beeped for the fourth checkpoint as I completed the turn.

"Good going, Jay." I could hear Vinnie holding back tears as he spoke on the radio.

I tightened my grip on the throttle handle as I headed for the fifth checkpoint. I caught up quickly to Russ, passing him the moment my GPS beeped. My name swapped places with his on the leaderboard screen, putting me in third place, right behind Ash. I was headed for the final turn. A quick check on the navigation screen revealed that Max had already finished the race and landed.

I flew straight towards the starting line checkpoint, accepting my position in third place for round two of this year's NJRA Nationals. A teardrop rolled down my cheek, followed by a couple more.

"Jet Racer Eight Zero." I sniffled, extending the flaps and landing gear. "Preparing for landing."

The tears kept coming. I started gagging as my throat tightened up. My stomach cramped up as I let out a mouthful of vomit all over my flight jacket.

"Jet Racer Eight Zero, you are clear for landing."

My throat was burning. I vomited again. The queasy feeling was gone. I flipped the switch to turn off the smoke system. My entire upper body ached as I began my descent.

Memories of Julianne flooded my brain again like a rising tide; her phoenix-orange nail polish that matched her plane, that floral blouse she always wore, all the movies we'd watched together, her reaction to Andrew's skill when he first arrived, and, just the night before, her taking all those photos of the food and ice sculptures at dinner.

The jolt of the wheels touching down shook me out of that thought-overwhelmed state. I took off my vomit-covered flight jacket and rolled it up with the clean side facing out. I opened the canopy and crumpled over the side of the plane, and the last of my stomach contents erupted onto the runway. With my left hand over my stomach and my rolled-up flight jacket under my right arm, I stumbled as my feet reached the ground.

There were no signs waving in the crowd. Everyone's eyes were fixed on the TV screen. Over and over, from different angles each time, a slow motion video showed the exact moment that Mathias's plane hit Julianne's. The crowd shouted louder with each replay. The screen showed Julianne's #10 falling in slow motion from the sky after being hit. The camera zoomed in on the plane as it hit the lake and was torn to pieces, just as I had seen with my own eyes.

I covered my face with my hand and turned away from the crowd and the flashes of the cameras. They were probably too focused on the screen to pay much attention to me. I walked around my plane toward the hangars. I was so used to hiding my feelings, always being told that "big boys don't cry". But now, just like the day I was taken from my birth parents' home, I could no longer hold back the tears.

"Jay," Vinnie blew his nose and then reached out to hug me. I opened my arms to him. "No shame in crying. It's a tough time for all of us."

"Sure is." Irene joined our hug. "I'm not usually an emotional person, but I am right now."

"Nothing to feel ashamed about." I sniffled.

"There was nothing any of us could've done," Vinnie added.

"I watched the whole thing happen," I said. "I had a perfect view of it all."

"You're going to be alright, Jay," Ash said, walking toward me. He gripped my hand. I guess he wasn't much of a hug person.

"Thanks," I replied.

"Don't be too hard on yourself, you gave it everything you got," Irene said. She always tried to find a way to cheer me up.

CHAPTER 10

I continued walking along the runway, my throat still burning and my stomach still cramping. I heard someone running behind me approaching quickly. I turned around and saw the shadow of Max looming over me.

"You killed her! You're going to get it," Max shouted, grabbing both of my arms.

I tried to pull away from him, but I knew I had no chance against someone his size.

"You son of a bitch, you did this just to mess with me!" he screamed, stomping his foot on the ground.

"I had nothing to do with it," I said, trying to stay calm.

"You wanted her dead so I'd stop hitting on her," he shouted.

I managed to take a step backward and stumbled, losing my balance.

He pinned me against the hangar wall. "You just don't know what it's like to love a girl, do you?" He had a point there. I really didn't know what it was like to love a girl.

I froze. I remembered what Ms. Ritchie, my high school social worker, had said years ago about how being mad back at someone who's already angry at you doesn't help anyone in the situation. I was never the type of person who liked to pick fights. In fact, I didn't even like to get angry if I didn't have to; not even when I was being held down by a guy an entire foot taller and at least a hundred pounds heavier than me.

But I couldn't believe that Max blamed me for what happened to Julianne. "I swear I didn't do anything."

Deep down, I knew it was useless to reason with him at that point.

He pulled a small can of WD-40 out of his flight jacket pocket and waved it in front of me. "Then what the hell was *this* doing near *your* plane?"

Did he fly the entire race with that in his pocket?

"How could anyone have used that to mess with her?" I said.

"I don't know, to loosen up parts? To unbolt her seat?" He popped the cap off the can and sprayed it in my face. I managed to shut my eyes before the cold spray hit me, but the smell made me nauseous. "Don't even try to lie!"

"Max, stop!" He only leaned tighter against me. It was getting harder to breathe by the second.

"You stop denying it!"

"I swear to God I didn't do anything," I shouted. I craned my neck, trying to wipe the WD-40 off my face with the collar of my shirt.

"You think I'd believe you were just fixing a squeaky door?" I could feel all his weight leaning against me.

Out the corner of my eye, I saw a few TV cameras pointed at us. I could hear the cheering of the crowd growing louder and louder in the background, as if the fans were kids crowding around a school fight. I buried my nose into my collar to block out the smell of WD-40.

"You saw it, didn't you?" he shouted, easing his pressure on me.

Saw the whole crash with my own eyes? Yes. I took a deep breath. I could almost taste the WD-40 on my tongue.

He took a few steps back and threw the can on the ground. "Tell me what you saw. Now!"

I wiped my face with my sleeve. "I-I-I-I," I stuttered, trying to recall the scene. "I saw Mathias's plane hit her and then—"

"And then what?" he snapped. Sweat dripped from his forehead. His face had turned completely red.

And then what? I had wondered the exact same thing.

"Maybe she passed out? I have no idea," I replied, shrugging.

"Passed out? I don't think so." He grabbed me by my shirt collar. I jerked backwards, trying to get out of his grasp. "Tampered with, that's what!"

Max pinned me against the hangar wall again. It felt as though all of his weight was crushing me like a slow-motion flyswatter on a fly. Tears began to stream down my face as my entire body went weak.

"Go on, keep crying. The *cameras* are on you," Max taunted. I didn't care that I was being watched. I had every right to be upset and angry. I mean, who wouldn't be in this situation?

"Stop blaming your problems on me!" I screamed,

THE JET RACER

letting the tears run down my face and onto the sleeve of Max's flight jacket.

"It was planned!" He started to choke me.

I grabbed his hands to take the weight off my neck, digging my nails in as hard as I could in an attempt to make him let go.

"Somebody get security!" a voice shouted from nearby. Someone was running.

"Daddy!" a female voice cried from nearby. It sounded like a young teen. "Don't hurt him."

Max immediately let go of my neck and I dropped to the ground. I turned my head toward the voice; it was Izzy. It was the first time I'd ever seen her in person, but I recognized her from the photo Max hung in his room.

I peeled my shirt off and used it to wipe the rest of the WD-40 off my face. I could still smell the fumes of it, making me nauseous again. I crumpled up the shirt and tossed it away from me. *So long, lucky shirt.* As I sat on the ground in my undershirt, my sailboat tattoo was in full view for everyone to see, but I couldn't have cared less.

"Izzy, what are you doing?" Max said. He sounded slightly calmer at that point.

"Well, I wasn't going to stand there and let you beat him up like that." She had her hands on her waist.

"Just let me deal with it, okay?" He tried to grab my right hand, but Izzy snatched his hand away.

"Leave him alone, Dad!" she shouted.

"Jay here is the reason for what happened!" Max shot back, pointing at me.

ANDY DAVIDS

Two security guards in yellow safety vests approached the three of us. Max tried to shove them away but they were able to grab both of his arms. Screaming and shouting, he tried to break free, but he gave up after a few seconds. He began huffing and puffing as the guards escorted him away, his entire body slouched and his head down. A bunch of pit crew members ran toward me and Izzy.

"Jay," Izzy said holding my hand, "sorry about my dad there."

"It's okay, it's not your fault," I replied, sobbing. "What are you doing here, though? I thought you didn't like races."

"I don't. But it is the nationals and when I found out my dad was going to be flying, I thought I'd ask him for a ticket," she replied. "You're a great pilot, by the way."

So even Max's daughter thinks I am a great pilot.

"Thanks," I replied. I was flattered, even though I'd already been told that many times in the last two days. I could feel that my breathing had slowed down once I was safe. "But Vinnie's catching up."

"What did he spray on you?" She asked. "Engine oil? Smells nasty."

A security guard walked up to us. He seemed to be focused on Izzy.

"Excuse me, miss, where's your pass?"

"Uh, you mean this?" She pulled out an admission ticket from her pocket.

"Miss, you can't be here with that. Only racers and stadium staff allowed."

"But Max is my dad," she replied. "He tried to choke

163

Jay. Didn't you see?"

"Look, this is a restricted area." He pointed to a sign attached to the chain-link fence nearby. "You can't be here, you got that?"

"Alright, I'll go." She waved goodbye to me, then turned and followed the security guard.

I struggled to my feet and walked over to the first aid station. I didn't think I'd been too badly injured in that altercation, but thought I should get myself checked out anyways.

"Could you sit down for me?" the attendant asked. "I'm going to check for any bleeding, broken bones, or other injuries. Just let me know if anything hurts."

She took a look at my arms. They were covered in bruises. "Let me see the back of your neck."

I winced as I bent forward.

"A bit of bruising here," she said. "But glad you're safe."

She took out an instant ice pack from a first aid kit, squeezed it to activate it, and wrapped it with a paper towel. She then told me to hold it against wherever my body hurt for no more than twenty minutes at a time. I got up off the chair and thanked her, then walked out of the tent holding the ice pack against my throbbing neck.

A news reporter in a navy-blue suit was waiting outside the first aid station. A camera crew stood beside him.

"Hey, Jay, got a minute to answer a few questions?" he asked.

I could feel the familiar lump building up in my throat.

Not another interview. But there was no way I could break away without being rude. He handed me a wireless microphone.

"This is Trey Lawrence with ESPN and right now I am standing by with Jay Smith at the NJRA nationals," he introduced himself, looking into the camera, before turning to me.

"Jay, I heard from some of the other racers that because everything happened so quickly, nobody really had time to react to the situation."

"I was already pretty nervous coming in to the race today, after yesterday's finish in the first round." I paused for a second, trying to keep a straight face in front of the camera even though I could feel my eyes filling with tears. "I guess the first thing that came into my mind was 'What the…?' and then it was like 'Oh God, I hope she's alright.'"

"I can only imagine the shock you must've been in. Was it difficult for you to stay focused on the race?"

"They taught us in training camp how to stay calm and keep on flying when something bad happens to another pilot, even if it's someone from your own league. I mean, it's hard not to worry about them, but your own safety always comes first. So yes, I was fully aware that I was still in the race, and I still want to finish in first. But at the same time, I had to be careful and keep my eyes on my surroundings so I didn't end up in an accident too."

"How would you describe being right in the moment of it all, if you get what I mean?"

"It was sort of like something out of a movie, like how

they show an explosion in full detail," I replied. My entire body was heavy from the stress and exhaustion. I shifted toward the nearby hangar wall and leaned against it. "It almost felt like slow motion as I watched Julianne's plane hit the water below. There was a huge splash, and then suddenly there was debris floating all over the lake. It was like a crash on the highway, you know that the more you look at it, the more it'll bother you, but you just can't take your eyes off it."

"That is a good analogy, Jay. Was there anything else that really stuck out to you at the time?"

"Yes, the exact moment that her dot on my radar disappeared. But I kept telling myself that I was still in the race and I had to finish it."

"That must have been pretty intense. The last I heard from the officials, search teams are trying to recover both Julianne Madison and Mathias Stewart's black boxes from the lake. What do you feel will come from that?"

"They'll probably have some answers for what really happened, or at least I hope so."

"Thank you so much, Jay, for your time. Again, really sorry you had to see something like that happen to a fellow league member."

I could not help but tear up again. I turned around and walked quickly away without saying goodbye, but I looked back and waved at the reporter before heading into the racers' building. I headed straight for the bathroom. I tossed the ice pack in the garbage, and then threw my undershirt in too, as it smelled of WD-40. I stripped off the rest of my clothes and stepped into the shower.

"Juli, I'm sorry I ever looked down on you," I sobbed, letting the sound of the running water drown out my crying. I visualized Julianne as she'd been from the previous day, with her hair pulled back in a messy bun and her nails painted phoenix-orange to match her plane.

"You're a good pilot and a good friend too," I sobbed. "Remember when you asked me how I make my vertical loops?"

The memory of that conversation was stuck in my head.

"Jay, can you show me how you do such a nice vertical loop?" she'd said over the radio. "I could never get mine perfectly round."

"Sure, watch me," I'd said into my headset.

"You want to start with a steady pull back. Look to the left and watch your wingtip trace a circle on the horizon, then keep going until you're inverted. If you watch your wingtip as a guide, you should get a nice round loop."

"Sounds simple enough," she'd said. "Thanks, Jay."

I turned off the hot water. The shock of the cold water rushing out onto my face snapped me back to reality. My elementary school classmates' shouts of "Big boys don't cry" echoed at the back of my head, but still the intense rush of emotion made me drop to my knees on the shower floor. I buried my face in my hands and cried for what seemed like an eternity. My mind skipped to Ms. Ritchie telling me that it was okay to cry, especially in difficult times. "Trying to deny those feelings only does more harm than good," she'd said.

Finally, the tears stopped. I got back to my feet, turned off the tap, and stepped out of the shower. Shivering, I dried off and put my pants back on. I didn't have a clean shirt to change into, so I draped the towel around myself, then walked back to the men's sleeping quarters and put on a new T-shirt.

I felt an urge to see if I could find something of Julianne's to hold on to, something that would help me feel better about the fact that she wasn't there anymore. I stepped out of the men's sleeping quarters, turning my head left and right like I was about to cross a busy street. The hallway was clear. I peeked my head through the open door of the women's sleeping quarters to make sure nobody was around. Julianne's navy-blue suitcase sat next to one of the beds.

I spotted her makeup bag lying on the floor next to the suitcase. The white cotton blouse with grey flowers that she wore at dinner the night before hung from one of the bedposts. I grabbed the blouse, crumpling it up to fit into one of my cargo pockets, then picked up the makeup bag and stuffed it into my other pocket. There was something about that blouse that I was drawn to. It wasn't just the fact that Julianne had worn it. I wanted to wear it. I returned to the men's sleeping quarters and grabbed my NJRA hoodie, then headed back to the bathroom.

There was no one there. I went into one of the stalls and locked the door, then shut the toilet lid. I took off my shirt and hung it and my hoodie on the hook on the stall door. I took the floral blouse out of my pocket and put it on. Julianne was shorter than me, so the sleeves were a bit short, but I didn't mind. I had a feeling of butterflies in my stomach as I looked down and admired myself in the blouse. The smooth wispiness of the material gave me goosebumps, like the first time I'd tried on one of my adoptive mom's evening gowns. I blushed slightly as I sat down on the toilet lid. I ran my hand over the small ruffles around the collar and the grey floral design on the front of the blouse.

'What are you doing, Jayson? Boys don't wear flowers.' There was my adoptive mother's voice inside my head. It was the same voice that yelled at me every time I was caught sneaking into her closet and trying on her clothes and the same voice telling me that she had burned my socks with pink flowers on them. I never understood why she hated those socks so much, especially since I'd bought them from a menswear store.

I looked down at my hands. *My fingers could use some nail polish,* I thought. I pulled the makeup bag out of my pocket and placed it on top of the toilet paper holder. I examined the green and white polka-dot pattern on it. Then I flushed the toilet to muffle the sound of the zipper as I opened it. An unopened tube of eyeliner was at the top, but I just could not bring myself to try it. My last experience with eyeliner years ago resulted in my adoptive mom seeing me with a huge mess on my face in front of the bathroom sink.

There must be some nail polish. I rummaged through the bag, and indeed, there was some nail polish; a couple bottles, one of them phoenix-orange. I unscrewed the cap and painted my left thumbnail, keeping my hand over the makeup bag so no polish would drip onto my pants. I paused for a moment to admire my work, then painted the rest of the nails on that hand.

I remembered the image of David Bowie with his nails painted. I waved my hand in the air to help the polish dry faster, just like Julianne used to do when I'd watch her do her nails. I'd always wanted to ask her to do mine for me, but I was too afraid to.

I leaned over the makeup bag and dipped the brush into the bottle so I could paint the nails on my right hand. "Oh shit," I said out loud as the brush slipped from my shaky fingers. It flew up and hit my chin before landing on the makeup bag. My chin felt wet. I rubbed it with my finger, confirming that the wetness was nail polish and not just sweat.

I frantically screwed the cap back on the nail polish bottle and stuffed it back into the makeup bag.

I grabbed my T-shirt from the hook and put it on over the blouse, then put my NJRA hoodie on over the T-shirt so no ruffles would show through. I made sure to tuck the tails of the blouse into my pants. My heart was pounding. I really wanted to wash that nail polish off my face before anyone came in.

I flushed the toilet again before zipping the makeup bag closed. I stuffed it back into my pocket. As I unlocked the door, I realized that the entire bathroom smelled of nail polish. Or maybe it was the smell of WD-40 residue in my nose? I hoped the ventilation system would take care of it quickly.

I looked left and right before leaving the stall. The coast was clear. As I grabbed a bunch of paper towels from the dispenser and wet them under the tap, my phoenix-orange nails caught my eye. *Focus, Jay.* I looked in the mirror and started scrubbing the nail polish off my chin. I had to scrub until my skin was red to get it off.

A toilet flushed. I froze. I'd been sure there was no one else in the bathroom. I scrambled into one of the empty stalls and locked the door. Through the narrow space between the door and the wall, I caught a glimpse of someone washing his hands in the sink. It was Andrew. He picked up the wet paper towels I'd left on the edge of the sink and tossed them into the garbage on his way out.

I pulled my hoodie sleeve over my left hand as I left the bathroom. I paused to check the time on my phone.

"Hey, Jay." I recognized Irene's voice behind me.

"Hi, Irene," I replied, turning around.

"I was just about to go for a walk before dinner. Want to come?"

"Not really in the mood for it," I grumbled. I put my hand behind my back.

"C'mon, the fresh air and the outdoors will do you good."

"Alright," I replied. I had nothing better to do anyway. But first, I had to get rid of that makeup bag in my pocket. "Just have to drop something off in the sleeping quarters. Be right back."

There was nobody else in the men's sleeping quarters. I pulled the makeup bag out of my pocket and stuffed it under my pillow. Then I rejoined Irene in the hallway and followed her out of the racer's building. The gentle evening breeze tickled my face.

"How are you doing, Irene?" I asked. "Are you feeling alright?"

"I'm okay, but still in shock," she replied. "I can't believe she's gone."

"I haven't seen Vinnie since the race. I hope he's okay," I said.

"He said he needed some time alone."

Maybe I needed some time alone too, but at the same time, being around Irene was a good distraction from everything on my mind.

"He just needs a bit of time to process everything," Irene explained. "But let's not focus on that now."

She gestured for me to look toward the valley and the mountains beyond. There was not a cloud in the sky.

"Have you ever seen the valley and the mountains like that?" She took a deep breath of fresh air.

"No, I haven't. They sure are magnificent."

"You should enjoy the outdoors more," she said. "Back when I was in university, my school was literally on top of a mountain. In the fall, I would sit outside on the balcony of my residence just as the sun was starting to set and I'd look at all the beautiful colours. I lived on the top floor, and when it got dark, I would look up at the night sky and see all the stars. I've even seen a shooting star zooming through the sky until it was completely burned up."

"That sounds incredible. When I was little, I always wanted to see a shooting star so I could make a wish, but I never did."

"I can only imagine what the sunsets look like here in the fall," she replied, pointing to the horizon. "The entire valley glowing with gold and yellow and orange as the sun fades behind the mountains."

I could feel the tears coming again, though this time they were more like tears of happiness brought on by Irene's beautiful descriptions of sunsets and the night sky. I wiped my face on my hoodie sleeve, forgetting that I was trying to hide the nails on my left hand.

"It's okay, Jay," Irene said, patting me on the back. "I know you're holding back because you're afraid to cry."

My sniffles turned to sobs.

"You were probably told you shouldn't cry and should just man up instead," she said. I could see the glint of a tear in her eyes.

"Yes, many times," I sobbed. "I've been bullied so many times for being too sensitive."

"All humans cry, Jay. It doesn't matter whether you're male, female, gay, straight, butch, femme, or whatever. We all have feelings and they make us who we are. Having them doesn't mean you're weak."

I nodded, wiping my eyes on my sleeve again before reaching out to hold her hand.

"Are you wearing Julianne's blouse?"

My face turned red and my heart had skipped a beat.

Deep down, I knew she probably wouldn't say anything negative about it, but the fact that she had noticed caught me off guard. My first impulse was to say it was just her imagination, but I was never the best at lying. I always got caught.

"Uh... how did you know?"

"Saw it sticking out of your sweatshirt."

"I, uh ..." I took a breath. The blouse must have come untucked. I tucked it back in.

"Floral patterns sure suit you well." She glanced at my left hand. "Your nails look great too. That colour suits you."

She'd caught me red-handed, or rather, orange handed. But it felt as though all the weight on me had suddenly lifted.

"Thanks. I always wanted to paint my nails," I said. "Used to sneak into my mom's room and try all her makeup."

"And I guess she wasn't happy about it?"

"She'd literally scream at me every time she caught me," I explained. "Of course, that didn't stop me from stealing a lipstick from the dollar store when I was in junior high because I was too nervous to deal with the cashiers."

"I don't blame you for that. I was never into makeup and dresses, but nobody in my family really cared. A masculine woman like me is more widely accepted than a feminine man."

"You're right. I remember learning in history class how women fought for the right to wear pants. But men never fought for the right to wear dresses."

"My parents usually bought me clothes from the boys'

department anyway, because they didn't wear out as fast as girls' clothes. I played with toy cars and action figures and rode my skateboard around the neighbourhood, and I loved every minute of it. When Christmas came around, my parents would almost fall over laughing at the dress-up dolls and stuff I got from relatives, and then we'd return them with the gift receipts. But when I was sixteen, my grandparents from Hong Kong came to visit. They hadn't seen me since I was a baby. Of course they had to ask if I had a boyfriend."

"What did you say?"

"I just said 'Actually, I like girls.'" Despite her confident words, her voice was starting to tremble.

"And what did they think?"

"They said that I just hadn't found the right guy yet. I don't really talk to them anymore. But my parents were mad when they realized it wasn't just a phase. My dad was all like, 'How could you do this to us?' My mom just ignored me for the next few days. Eventually, she said that she still loved me no matter what."

"That's good, because you're always going to be her daughter. Did your dad change his mind too?"

"Living in San Francisco, we were used to seeing the queer community. But one day my dad caught me at a bar in the Castro District hitting on a girl. He's a paramedic, so he was responding to a call next door to the bar." She seemed to be choosing her words carefully. "I was really in trouble then, as I had used a fake ID to get in."

She seemed lost in thought for a moment. Then she said, "By the way, would you mind if I use your nail polish?"

THE JET RACER

You mean Julianne's nail polish, right?

I couldn't really imagine Irene wearing nail polish, but I guess she wanted to wear it as a tribute to Julianne.

"Not at all," I replied, smiling.

CHAPTER 11

I tapped my key card on the scanner to return to the racer's building after finishing my walk with Irene outside the stadium. I definitely felt calmer after the fresh air, the change of scenery, and the opportunity to let out some of that emotion.

"Coming to dinner?" I asked her.

"Going to have a shower first," she replied. "Be there in a bit."

In the dining hall, I picked up my dinner from the buffet line and took a seat at an empty table. I looked down at the fistful of salad on my plate and mindlessly flipped over a slice of tomato with my fork as I waited for Irene. I picked at my salad, looking toward the doorway every few minutes to see if she had arrived. Fifteen minutes passed with no sign of her. The clattering of plates being taken off the stack at the buffet line and the dull mumble of conversations filled the room as I looked at the empty seat on the other side of the table. I guess Irene needed some time to herself too.

I finished my dinner and placed my plate, glass, and cutlery into the tub of dirty dishes at the end of the buffet table. As I stepped out of the dining hall, I heard my name being called:

"Jayson David Smith."

A man a bit taller than me with greying hair stood next to the doorway. He was wearing a grey suit with a blue tie. *He's definitely some kind of NJRA official.*

"I need to talk with you." There was a strong air of authority in his voice; it reminded me of a teacher who was about to give me detention. "Come with me."

"What is it for?" I asked, my eyes widening.

"My name is Dr. Allen and I am an aviation medical examiner for the NJRA," he said, reaching out to shake my hand. My hand was trembling as I shook his. "I'll be conducting an assessment to ensure that you're still fit to fly, as per standard operating procedure following a major incident."

I followed Dr. Allen down the hallway into an office not too far from the leisure room. *So that's what these empty offices are for.* He sat down at the desk and I sat across from him. There was an empty chair next to his. I wondered for a moment if someone else would be joining him.

The silver name tag on his jacket said "Christopher Allen, M.D." and below it was the NJRA logo. There was an open file folder on the desk with my name printed on it, just like the kind you would see at a doctor's office. But there was no examination table in the middle of the room or medical instruments hanging on the wall. Several forms were spread out on the folder: my vaccination records, past eyesight and hearing test results, as well as reports from my yearly physical.

There was also a box of tissues next to the file folder; I had a feeling I was going to need those.

"I want you to answer all questions as honestly as possible," Dr. Allen explained. He took out a tablet from his briefcase under the desk and switched it on. "If you're unclear about something, please ask."

I felt like a prisoner in an interrogation room, surrounded by plain white walls on all four sides. It seemed like he was watching my very eye movements, my slightest facial expressions, and gestures as he was explaining.

"Before we start, can you state your full name?"

I took a deep breath. "Jayson David Smith."

"Alright. Have you felt at all like you were losing touch with reality since the end of the race today? Have you felt like you were seeing or hearing anything that wasn't there?" His voice was completely flat, almost robotic. It was not at all like talking to Ms. Ritchie, as that sense of compassion and understanding was missing.

"Well, the whole crash felt like it was a bad dream or something," I paused, trying to recall every single detail of the scene. The soft hum of the fluorescent lights filled the silence.

"Do you remember if you were aware that it wasn't a dream at the time?" he asked.

"Oh, I definitely knew it was real. And once I touched down on the runway, not seeing Julianne's and Mathias's planes come in for landing definitely confirmed that." It felt like Julianne's blouse was getting tighter under my hoodie.

"Can you describe what was going on inside your mind at the time of the incident?"

"Like in the air or after the race?" I asked.

"Right when you saw Julianne's plane go down."

"I remember that I kept wanting to look away, but I just couldn't. I wanted to make sure she was alright. I had to remind myself that there was still a race going on and that I had to finish it, no matter what else was happening."

I could feel the hairs on the back of my neck standing up with every tap of his fingers typing. I could see that he was only typing the important words, just like I used to do when I was taking notes in ground school.

"So, I had this tunnel vision, concentrating on reaching the finish line," I added, trying not to stutter as I spoke. "I knew that even if I was just going to quit instead of finishing the race, I still had to focus on getting back to the runway and making the landing."

"Since the incident this afternoon, do you remember any instances where you felt like you were scared for no particular reason?"

"I was definitely shocked when it happened," I said, trying to refresh my memory of how I'd felt at that moment. "I was fearing the worst."

"That's a natural response to a traumatic event. It starts off with shock because you haven't seen it coming and due to that, you enter a state of panic. Once that initial panic wears off, then you move into the grief stage. That's when you tend to focus more on the fact that that person is gone and on trying to come to terms with that."

I was worried that if he saw me shed a single tear, I would be banned from flying in the final round. I turned my head to the blank wall to my left and tried to envision my birth father, his six-foot, 250-pound frame towering over me, a faded black baseball cap on his balding head and a cartoon speech balloon next to his mouth saying, *GROW A PAIR*. I could almost hear those words in the deep, intimidating voice he'd used when he threatened to beat me when I couldn't stop crying.

Dr. Allen's voice snapped me back into the moment like the cold shower water hitting my face. "Do you remember any other feelings you had after watching Julianne's plane hit the water?"

"I felt sick to my stomach. I ended up puking like three times, first in the plane all over myself, then after I got out of the plane, and again when I was out on the runway." The nausea returned as I explained. That burning feeling in my throat was back. My eyes darted around the room in search of a garbage bin in case I needed to throw up again. *Grow a pair.*

"It's not uncommon to vomit after psychological shock. Extreme emotional responses can create a strong response in the nervous system that affects the stomach and therefore makes you vomit."

"I can't remember any other time I've been so scared to the point of throwing up, n-n-not even when I was first taken away by social services as a kid." I couldn't tell what was making me tear up more, the fact that Julianne was gone or the childhood memories coming up. I felt a couple teardrops escape and roll down my face. I grabbed a tissue from the box and wiped my eyes. *Grow a pair.*

"It's okay. Do you need a few minutes?" he asked,

typing some more notes on his tablet, his voice still dry and monotone despite his words.

I struggled to focus on the mental image of my birth father as I wiped my eyes, but more tears escaped with every passing second. *So much for trying to hold it in.*

His tone shifted, it became more pressing. "We have limited time. We have to continue."

I nodded, gulping as I waited for him to give me the news that I would be barred from flying until further notice.

"Now, do you remember having any feelings of wanting revenge or retaliation against Mathias for hitting Julianne?" He looked up from his tablet.

"No, I don't even know if he hit Julianne on purpose or not." I thought I heard footsteps in the hallway outside. *How soundproof are these offices, really?*

"Have you had any thoughts about wanting to hurt Mathias in some way if you saw him?"

"No, I'm not the kind of person to hurt anyone," I answered. I blew my nose with a tissue. I was never even the kind of person to blame things on other people. "I was more concerned about Julianne than Mathias, to be honest. It was probably like only thirty seconds between him hitting Julianne and her plane crashing into the lake, but it felt much longer. I remember I was gripping the flight controls so tightly that my knuckles were white while I was waiting for her to eject."

"I can imagine. I'd like to ask, how would you describe your relationship with Mathias otherwise?"

"I've never really spoken to him."

"Not even in the sleeping quarters, in the hallway, or in

the dining hall?" he asked.

I was almost impressed at how he was able to keep his face and voice emotionless the whole time. I wondered how he felt when he got home at night after taking to racers about a deadly incident.

"Other than to say hi, no. I don't really know the East Coast racers, for the most part."

"Alright then." Dr. Allen paused his typing to look me right in the eyes. "Have you had any feelings of anger towards any other person since the incident?"

"Yeah, Max," I said. I cleared my throat, unsure what to say next. "Because of what he did to me and the fact that he's trying to blame it all on me."

"What makes you think he's trying to blame it on you?"

"Because he's been sexually attracted to Julianne since the first day of the season, and it's all he ever talks about," I explained, stomping my foot on the floor at the last word. "He knew I was sick of hearing about his fantasies. So he blamed me for sabotaging Julianne's plane just so he'd stop hitting on her. He found a can of WD-40 near my plane and said I'd used it to sabotage her plane."

"People act irrationally when they are emotional, and sometimes they'll put the blame on someone else so they can feel better about the whole situation," he explained, typing on his tablet.

"Because honestly, I had nothing to do with it. And besides, I just can't see how a can of WD-40 could cause an entire plane to crash," I replied, feeling as though some of the words were caught in my throat. *Maybe whoever was behind it sprayed it into the inner workings of her plane?*

"Whether it was a sabotage or not, or how it happened, isn't my main concern right now. My main concern is you and how you're handling the aftermath of it. I need to ask you, how have you been trying to deal with the situation?"

"If anything, I regret not getting to know her better since the beginning of the season. She never really talked to me all that much, but that doesn't mean I won't miss her."

"Have you tried to focus on savouring some of the memories you've had together, as a way of moving forward from the loss?"

"Yes, uh, I did my nails," I said, pointing to my left hand. "It's her favourite colour."

I didn't mention that I had actually used *her* nail polish, or the fact that I was wearing her blouse.

"I did notice the nails," he replied. There was a slight note of excitement in his voice. "You do a better job than my daughter. She makes a mess all over her hand."

"Thanks. Not bad for my first time, is it?" I could feel myself blushing at his compliment. It wasn't really my first time, as I'd once tried to paint my nails was with my adoptive mom's purple nail polish, but I'd knocked over the bottle and it ended up all over my hand.

"Seems like painting your nails helps you feel better," he said, taking down notes.

"I'd always wanted to paint them," I replied. "Sometimes I look down at my hands and feel like something's missing. I do have quite a bit of a feminine side. I used to sneak into my mom's room and try on all her makeup."

"Well, it's your body, so if it makes you feel good, paint them. Has anyone else seen them?"

"Other than you, just Irene. She said she liked them and wanted to paint hers too."

"That's good to hear," he said, his voice flat again.

"There is this one guy, though." I decided not to say Andrew's name out loud, in fear that Dr. Allen would interpret it as wanting revenge. "I don't think he'd take it too well."

"It sounds like you are well aware of and even accepting of your feminine side, but you're worried about what others think."

"Pretty much. I've never had the confidence to really show it in front of other people."

He finished typing the last of his notes and took a pen out of his briefcase. He uncapped the pen and scribbled a couple of lines on one of the pages in the file folder.

"Jayson," he said, recapping the pen. "On behalf of the NJRA, I declare that you are clear to fly. Do take good care of yourself tonight and try to rest well. Listen to music that you like, visit the spa, or have a chat with someone you trust."

"For sure. I went for a walk around the stadium with Irene earlier and we were admiring how incredible the valley and the mountains are. It made me realize how little time I've spent outside since I arrived here."

"Going for a walk is great, and the Salt Lake Valley is definitely a sight to behold. Keep in mind that because you have witnessed a traumatic event, you might find yourself feeling emotionally numb at times," he explained. "You might even feel sick to your stomach again. If you feel like you need to check in with me a couple hours or so before the race, I'll be around."

I nodded, trying to avoid eye contact with him, worried that I would either cry again or Dr. Allen would change his mind.

"If you do feel that it's becoming too much to handle tomorrow, there is nothing wrong with withdrawing from the race," he added.

His advice was kind, but he reminded me of a call centre agent reading off a script.

"Don't feel like you're weak or a quitter for doing so. Remember, what you feel is completely valid, so don't feel that you have to tough it out when you can't anymore. Your own health is more important than any race you fly."

"I guess you're right." I was determined not to withdraw from the race. It was the final round of the nationals after all, and I didn't think Julianne would want me to.

"Do you have any other questions for me?" he asked.

I shook my head no.

"I'm going to give you the number of the NJRA support line. Don't be afraid to call if you feel you need some emotional support." He handed me a business card printed with the words 'NJRA Members' Support Line' and below them, 'Here for you 24/7' and a phone number.

"Thank you."

"I believe there are some officials waiting to speak to you," he said as he stood up.

I could feel my heart start to pound. *What do they want*

from me? As Dr. Allen opened the door, I saw two NJRA officials waiting outside the office. They both had silver name tags on their shirts and one of them was carrying a tablet. It looked exactly like the one Dr. Allen had used. Dr. Allen gestured for the two them to come in.

One of the men sat down on one of the empty chairs across from me.

"Hi Jayson, my name is Lee and this is my colleague Warren."

Warren turned around to close the office door before sitting down in the other chair. "We're with the NJRA Health and Safety Committee."

"Nice to meet you." I replied, extending my right hand to shake both of their hands. I kept my left hand on my lap under the desk so they wouldn't see my nails. First it was an interview with a medical examiner and now the Health and Safety Committee.

"We're going to ask you some questions. I know you are a bit distressed right now and some of the questions may be emotionally intense. But please keep in mind that this is important and as such, we require your cooperation," Warren explained.

"From what you saw in the weeks leading up to the race, did you notice any drastic changes in Julianne Madison's behaviour?" Lee asked. As Warren began typing notes on his tablet, his fingers made the same tapping sound on the screen that Dr. Allen's had.

"Honestly, she didn't really talk to me that much," I replied. "I mean, I only knew her for less than a year."

"What did she usually do in her spare time?"

I couldn't help but wonder how that question was relevant, but it probably was, or else he wouldn't have asked me. It wasn't like he just wanted to start a conversation with me.

"She really liked watching movies," I said, distracted by the rhythmic sound of Warren typing. "Either on her laptop or on the movie channel. She'd watch movies that she'd seen already over and over again."

"Did she do anything within the last week that she didn't normally do?"

"She went to an introductory rock climbing class that a sponsor invited her to. I don't think that's something she would normally do." I paused. "She liked to try new things a lot, though."

"Have you had any contact with Mathias Stewart in the last couple of days?"

"I haven't spoken to him at all." I wasn't sure whether it was the air conditioning in the office or Warren's frantic typing that was giving me chills.

"In situations like this, there's always a possibility of human error. From what you have seen, what did you feel about Julianne's attitude towards personal safety, particularly when it came to flying?"

"She seemed to have a pretty good attitude toward safety, both while flying at the league's airfield and at races, for as long as I've known her."

"It has been brought to our attention that a can of WD-40 was found in one of the hangars right next to your plane—"

"But why would that be suspicious in a hangar?" I interrupted, raising my eyebrows. "Isn't it something that pit crews would use?"

"NJRA policies require that anyone working in stadium hangars sign out all tools and supplies before they use them and sign them back in when finished. Do you remember when you first noticed the can there?" Lee asked.

"I don't remember seeing it when I was in the hangar before the race," I answered. "In fact, I don't think I saw it until Max sprayed it in my face after the race."

"Alright, that's all we need from you," Warren said as he finished typing the last of his notes. "Do you have any questions?"

"Yes, do you know if Max will be flying tomorrow?"

"That's between him and the medical examiner. We're not allowed to talk about it for confidentiality reasons. Is there anything else?"

I didn't know whether I was more concerned for Max or for myself, knowing what he was really capable of. At the same time, if he wasn't fit to fly, it would mean I had a much better chance to take first place.

I shook my head. Warren turned off his tablet. He and Lee stood up at the same time. My feelings of uneasiness were replaced by calmness the moment the two of them stepped out the door. I left the office and closed the door behind me. I returned to the men's sleeping quarters to grab the nail polish for Irene. Russ was sitting on his bed with his laptop, too focused on what he was doing to pay any attention to me as I slid the makeup bag out from under my pillow. Besides, he had his headphones on. I unzipped the bag, took out the nail polish, and stuffed it into my hoodie pocket.

Then I grabbed my toiletries kit and made my way down the hallway to the bathroom. I walked over to the sinks to brush my teeth. Vinnie was washing his face at one of the sinks.

"How're you feeling, Jay?" he asked.

"Better, knowing that I'm clear to fly tomorrow. You?"

"Did you just finish talking to Dr. Allen?"

I nodded, taking my toothbrush and toothpaste out of my toiletries kit.

"Same here. That's why I wasn't at dinner, but I'm clear to fly." He gave me a thumbs up in the mirror.

"Aren't you worried about Max?" I asked.

"Well, if he wins, he wins. At least I tried," he replied.

"I mean, it is sad what happened today, but now that I've had a chance to get it out, I feel better."

"Yeah, I had my chance to cry too," he said. "If you want to talk about it more, I'll be in the sleeping quarters."

I turned on the faucet to wash my face.

Vinnie paused, looking at my nails. "By the way, did you paint your nails?"

"Yes, I did," I said, pulling the bottle out from my hoodie pocket to show him. I couldn't stop myself from blushing a bit. But like everyone had said to me that day, it was nothing to be ashamed of. "Irene said she'd paint her nails too. I have to give this to her. Catch you in a bit."

"You might want to hold on to that when she's done.

I'm almost thinking I want to paint my nails too. Or maybe I should let you do them for me." He smiled.

I went over to the women's sleeping quarters to see if Irene was there. I waited a couple minutes before I saw her walking out of the women's bathroom towards me.

"Irene, here you go," I said, handing her the bottle of nail polish.

"Thanks," she replied.

"Have a good night."

Back in the men's sleeping quarters, Vinnie was on his laptop. He looked up at me as I walked over to him.

"Tired?" he asked.

"Yeah, but I don't feel like sleeping." I looked up at the clock; it was only 9:35 p.m. "It's not even ten yet."

"Just sending my condolences to Juli's family," he said.

"That's wonderful of you." Again, I felt like the words were stuck in my throat.

"When I'm done I'll search for some science docs for us to watch."

As I waited for Vinnie to finish his emails, I noticed the Bruce Dickinson book on his bed next to his pillow. *What if Max walks in and sees that I've lent his book to Vinnie?*

"Vinnie," I whispered to him. "Is it okay if I take the Bruce Dickinson book back tonight?"

"Sure, no problem." He handed it to me and continued typing. "It's definitely an interesting read, but I can get back to it another time."

I went over to my bed and put the book next to my pillow. I kind of wanted to read a bit more of it before going to sleep, but I decided it would be better to spend time with Vinnie, since we were both still hurting from everything that had happened.

Vinnie put on a documentary about supermassive black holes and the mysteries of the universe. I found myself getting absorbed pretty quickly, even though a lot of that scientific stuff was way over my head. Everything that had happened that day with Julianne, then Max, seemed to melt away as I struggled to keep up with all the scientific information.

"Do you really understand all this, Vinnie?" I asked.

"I've seen it a couple times," he replied. "It took some getting used to, that's for sure."

Max walked into the sleeping quarters while we were watching the documentary. My heart was pounding, even though he paid no attention to either of us or to anyone else in the room for that matter. I pretended not to notice him and so did Vinnie.

CHAPTER 12

"A little too close for comfort there, Jay!" Vinnie shouted over the radio.

I looked at my navigation screen and noticed that my red dot was quickly catching up to his. I was headed directly toward his tail. I couldn't let myself crash into him. *I need to get away from him.*

The edges of our dots were beginning to overlap on the navigation screen. I jerked the control stick to the left, but it wouldn't budge. I stomped my feet on both rudder pedals — they had suddenly malfunctioned. I had no choice but to eject. I reached under my knees for the ejection handle. It was missing.

What has it all come to now? I continued scrambling for the ejection handle. The crunch of metal filled the cockpit. I could feel my bones cracking as my body was flooded with intense pain, as though an elephant had stepped on my back. Then everything went pitch black.

Something hit my forehead. I opened my eyes and lifted the Bruce Dickinson book off my face. In the dim light of the room, my nails glowed faintly. Phoenix-orange, Julianne's favourite colour. There was a cold feeling against my back. I had rolled off my bed onto the hardwood floor in the middle of the night, blanket, pillow, book, and all.

I sat up and threw the blanket and pillow back onto the bed. I placed the book back beside my pillow where it had been the night before. I stood up. Vinnie was still sleeping in the bed to my right; Russ was still in asleep in his bed as well. *What a relief I didn't wake them or anyone else, for that matter.*

It was completely dark outside. It must have been around two or three in the morning. I climbed back onto my bed and lay there, staring up at the ceiling, trying to go back to sleep. It had all been just a dream.

After tossing and turning for a few hours, I got dressed, brushed my teeth, washed my face, and arrived at the dining hall for breakfast. In the hallway, a member of the pit crew handed me back my flight jacket. It looked almost as good as new. There was not a single bit of WD-40 residue or vomit on it, not even a hint of the smell. I picked up my breakfast from the buffet and joined Vinnie and Irene at their table.

"Sleep alright last night?" Vinnie asked, shooting me a look of concern. "You rolled onto the floor apparently."

"Did I wake you up?"

"Heard a loud thud next to me, looked over, and saw you on the floor," he explained. "Looked like you were okay so I went back to sleep."

"Well, I had a bad dream," I replied.

"Oh, did you see me naked or something?" He smiled.

"Or rather, did you see *me* naked?" Irene added with a smirk.

This is getting too awkward.

I walked out to the hangar a few hours later. All of the racers' planes were lined up on the starting line. Other racers were in the area getting ready for the race. Members of the pit crew were polishing the exteriors of the planes. There was a stripe of black tape on the tailfin of my plane; Irene's and Vinnie's both had the same stripe. Max's probably had it too, but it was hard to see with its all black livery. I looked closer at the tape on my plane's tailfin. A corner was coming loose. I rubbed it so that it wouldn't fly off during the race.

"How're you two feeling?" Irene asked.

"Oh, I'm pumped up," Vinnie replied with gusto. "I'm going to kill it up there."

Irene gave him a high five.

"Much better," I replied.

"Just fly and don't think too much," Irene said.

I nodded, but I could still feel the butterflies in my stomach.

It was strange seeing seventeen instead of twenty planes and knowing one of the three missing was gone for good.

Max walked right past us on his way out of the hangar. He paid no attention to us whatsoever, just like he'd ignored me and Vinnie watching science documentaries in the sleeping quarters the night before. He seemed surprisingly calm compared to when I'd seen him after the previous day's race.

"Break a leg, Jay," Ash said, shaking my hand.

Now that I'd had some time to calm down and spend

with friends, I was feeling better about the race.

"Folks, we are now on the third and final adrenaline-packed round of the NJRA Nationals. My name is Jack Davids and I will be your host. As we can see, the tailfins of the planes from Northern Washington's Central City Jet Racing League's members have been marked with a black stripe, the NJRA symbol of mourning for a fellow league member. Recapping from yesterday's race, we saw an incredible performance from Wyoming's Ash Christie." The crowd cheered as Ash's name was announced. "Both Erikson and Smith, also fan favourites, seem to have a good chance at first prize, although Giaconia looks to be another likely contender. To start off the event, we will have Lauren Christie, Ash Christie's daughter, present the national anthem."

A blonde-haired girl in a sleeveless, knee-length white dress strode out to the runway. Her dress reminded me of the ones that Julianne used to wear when it was really hot out. Her hair was chin-length and slightly curly. It was the first time I'd seen her, and I could not quite see a resemblance to her father.

Jack Davids's voice boomed over the loudspeaker again. "Lauren has been singing since she was five and has performed at several festivals and state fairs. At only seventeen years old, she'll be releasing her first full-length album this October. Ladies and gentlemen, please rise and remove your hats. Before we begin singing the national anthem, we will take a moment of silence."

The crowd went silent. I just wasn't going to cry in front of the crowd, but when I looked down the line, I saw tears running down other racers' faces. Members of the pit crew went down the line with boxes of tissues. I was overpowered with memories of Julianne as I reached for a tissue. *It's okay to cry,* I told myself. *Even with everyone watching; even with cameras facing us.*

After a moment, Lauren began to sing.

Looking up at the Jumbotron, I could see that the silver cross around her neck was quite tarnished. It wasn't reflecting the light from the sun above. She must have gotten it from one of those street vendors at the beach.

After Lauren left the area, Jack began announcing the racers' names over the PA system. The crowd cheered at both Max's name and mine. *Looks like he's clear to fly after all.*

"The planes have been oiled and fuelled, and now, we are about to find out who will be this year's national champion," Jack announced. "The racers are ready to give it their all for a place on the podium!"

As I settled into the pilot's seat of #80, I shut the canopy, dampening the cheering of the crowd. I switched my radio on and, when it was my turn, said my racer number, as did everyone else on the starting line. I could see Max's black #67 to the left of Irene's red #52, and to the left of Max's, Vinnie's blue #37.

"Racers, start your engines."

Fly like Bruce Dickinson, I said to myself. That immediately brought Max into my head, but I decided to focus all my frustrations from everything that had happened the previous day on the race ahead of me.

I heard the familiar rumble of my engine starting up.

THE JET RACER

The starting horn went off. Smoke system on, brakes released, flaps set, throttle to full. I lifted off from the runway. A teal-coloured plane rushed ahead of me from my right as I headed for the first turn of the figure-8 course. I didn't need to look at the number on the tailfin to know that it was #45, Sara Reyes, the woman Irene had been making out with at the kickoff party. My GPS beeped as I flew over the second checkpoint.

Less aileron, less aileron. My right hand tightened on the control stick as I completed the pylon turn. The GPS beeped for the third checkpoint. I was pretty much at Sara's tail now, and I caught a glimpse of Irene's plane not too far ahead. I couldn't see the tailfin number from my angle, but the black stripe on the red tail was a giveaway.

I loosened my grip on the control stick as I levelled out from the banked turn. My GPS beeped as I flew over the fourth checkpoint. It did not take much to pass Sara, and I soon found myself on the tail of Irene's plane. I kept my speed up and continued flying toward the fifth checkpoint, passing Irene easily. My GPS beeped for the checkpoint.

Irene seemed to be flying slower than I would have expected. It was almost like she had let me pass, just like that. I then heard what sounded like sobbing through the radio.

"Jet Racer Eight Zero to Jet Racer Five Two, everything ok?"

There were no words, only more sniffling.

I tried to stay focused on the race. My GPS beeped twice as I passed over the starting line at full speed, indicating the start of the second lap.

"Jet Racer Five Two to Tower," Irene sobbed.

What is she doing?

I eased back on the throttle slightly as I headed for the turn at the bottom right corner of the figure-8 course. Back to full speed after the turn, I closed in on Russ's plane.

"Requesting for landing. Withdrawing from race."

I could hear that she was really struggling to hold back the tears in that sentence. I watched on my navigation screen as her dot travelled off the course and back towards the starting line.

Maybe I should quit too, I thought. But I knew Julianne wouldn't want that. *No, I won't give up that easily. Don't think anymore. Just fly. Fly, Jay, fly. Do it for Julianne.*

I was right on Russ's tail as I approached the pylon turn. The GPS beeped for the third checkpoint. The reflection of the lake below caught my eye, but I tried to keep my focus on the race at hand. I swore that, for a moment, I could hear the sound of Julianne's #10 hitting the surface of the lake over the rumble of the engine.

My train of thought was broken by my GPS beeping for the fourth checkpoint. My knuckles went white as I tightened my grip on the control stick again and made the turn, slamming the throttle forward as soon as I levelled out. I felt the power of the afterburners working, as the roar of the engine surrounded me. I passed another racer, but I paid no attention to the cockpit or the number on the tailfin.

I switched my radio over to the commentator's channel. The GPS beeped as I flew over the fifth checkpoint.

"With Chan's withdrawal from the race, Reyes of SoCal

Jet Racing League has moved up to seventh place, and now she's quickly catching up to Smith. We haven't really seen much from her this season, though she's definitely got it. Up on the top three, it looks like Giaconia has just taken third place from Stevenson. Man, that rookie is definitely something! He's not far behind Taylor who is in second and Lorenzi leading the race, two of the three pilots from New York City Jet Racing League!"

I switched back to the racers' channel and glanced at the leaderboard screen to confirm what I had just heard. I was in sixth place. I was surprised that Vinnie had made his way up to the top three already; it was only the second lap.

I flew straight for the starting line at full speed with no other planes in my way. My GPS beeped three times to indicate the third lap.

I wonder where Max is. I hadn't seen any sign of him yet, and his name wasn't anywhere near the top three on the leaderboard. That was just as surprising as Vinnie being third so early in the race. I watched as Vinnie's name swapped places with Robert Taylor's, only to switch back a couple seconds later.

I switched my radio back to the commentator's channel.

"It looks like Erikson's getting a bit too close to Reyes for comfort as he makes the pass. What a risky move! He's really picking up speed and closing the gap on Smith!"

My heart skipped a beat when I heard my name. Max was now right in front of me, in sixth place and me in seventh, with only two other racers between him and Vinnie. I fell into a state of tunnel vision as I struggled to focus on the upcoming pylon turn and catch up to Max. Suddenly, Max veered toward the mountains at the edge of the valley.

What the hell is Max doing? Does he want to get himself disqualified?

"Tower to Jet Racers Six Seven and Eight Zero, this is a judge's warning. Our systems show that you have flown off course. Please turn around and continue from checkpoint three," the air traffic controller said over the radio.

I was so focused on following him that I had flown off course as well. Max paid no attention and continued flying toward the mountains.

At that point, I just didn't want to fly in the race anymore. I might as well follow Max to see why he was going so far off-course. I looked down at my navigation screen. There were no other red dots nearby, even though Max was right in front of me.

"Get your ass back here," Ray, the third racer from New York City, said. "Right now!"

"Get back in the race!" Ash shouted. "Listen to everyone!"

"Everything okay there?" Sara asked. "Max?"

"His radio might be off." Vinnie sounded rather frantic.

"Tower to Jet Racer Six Seven, do you read me? Please respond if you do. This is an official order."

Why would he turn his radio off? He had it on at the beginning of the race.

"Tower to Jet Racer Eight Zero, do you read me? I repeat, this is an official order. You are required to comply in order to avoid further action."

"Jay, get back in the race!" Vinnie's voice shouted over the radio. It caught my attention. I wanted to listen to Vinnie because I cared about him, but I just could not bring myself to turn around.

Julianne rushed into my mind, like water from a stream into the ocean. Her asking how I did my vertical loops on her first day at the league, her love of movies, the colour of her hair, and her signature orange nail polish, which I was still wearing on my left hand as it gripped the throttle lever. A warm, comfortable, and familiar feeling wrapped itself around me like a velvety blanket.

I was now flying parallel to Max.

"Tower to Jet Racers Six Seven and Eight Zero, you have been disqualified from the race for refusing to obey official orders. Please return to the runway and land."

I couldn't bring myself to turn back and I couldn't understand why. I could have just left Max out there and let the NJRA deal with him. I wanted to switch my radio to the commentator's channel just to see what Jack Davids was saying, but I didn't know how I would react.

"Tower to Jet Racers Six Seven and Eight Zero, this is a warning. You have five minutes to bring yourselves back toward the runway and prepare for landing or we will disable your flight controls and activate your remote autopilot function."

So that's what happens when racers fly off course and refuse to return.

I looked over at Max's plane. I could see his face

through the bubble canopy. He was definitely conscious, sitting upright with his headset cap on. He showed no reaction to any of the warnings; most likely, he had turned off his radio. His left hand was gripping the throttle with only three fingers, just like he always did.

He turned his head and looked me right in the eyes. I could see the look of burning fire in them. Before I knew it, his plane whipped toward my left wing like a black shadow rushing through the air. I heard a loud crack and a chunk of solid grey metal flew right past me. I felt the plane shaking out of control. My jaw dropped as I realized what that chunk of metal was. It was my plane's left wing.

My altitude alarms were blaring and my warning lights were flashing. I quickly pulled up on the control stick, trying to get out of Max's way. I had never felt panic like this in my entire life. I just wanted to squeeze my eyes shut.

Take a deep breath, Jay.

My heart was beating so fast that it felt like it could explode any second. I didn't know how many minutes had passed since the last warning over the radio, but I found myself crossing my fingers while gripping the controls, hoping they would activate my remote autopilot and guide me to landing safely. But then had I realized that the remote autopilot wouldn't be of much use given the state of my plane.

Deep breath, Jay, deep breath.

"Mayday, mayday, mayday!" I shouted into the headset, panting between each *mayday*. "Jet Racer Eight Zero to Tower, I have no choice but to eject."

I needed to tell them or else they wouldn't know where to find me in the desert.

"Tower copy."

I was still panic-stricken. Every single hair on my body was standing up. Should I eject, or would the remote autopilot be able to save me even with my plane's left wing ripped off?

"Jet Racer Eight Zero to Tower, I am ejecting in three... two... one..."

I reached behind the headrest and yanked the face shield over my head. I let go of the controls and reached between my knees, fumbling for the ejection handle. My altitude warning signal was blaring non-stop, louder by the second. With my hands wrapped around the outer handle, I squeezed the inner handle of the two-stage mechanism, and then jerked the whole assembly upwards with every last bit of energy I had.

No turning back now.

The clear acrylic canopy popped right off as the shock of the explosive charges shook my entire body. It felt like an atomic bomb had gone off inside me. I glanced around the cockpit of #80 one last time before I felt the intense wind blast. A sharp ringing, similar to a fire alarm, filled my ears, drowning out the sounds in my headset and every other outside noise. As I was propelled upwards, my eyelids were forced shut. My legs would have been flailing around if it were not for the restraints that had deployed on the ejection seat.

Twelve times Earth's gravity, as they said in ground school. No wonder it felt like my body weighed a thousand pounds as I was launched out of the cockpit. No wonder it felt like I was being ripped apart, limb by limb, or spaghettified, like I was passing through the event horizon of a black hole.

So this is what it's come to.

A sense of complete calm and peace washed over me. I no longer felt like I was being ripped apart. The vibrations of the rocket motor seemed to disappear. It felt like someone had wrapped a warm, fuzzy blanket around me or I was sitting on the front porch of Central City Jet Racing League airfield on a warm summer morning.

I felt my whole body yanked straight upwards like a puppet on a string. My eyelids felt heavy. I tried to look up but my neck was stiff. I could not turn my head in any direction without electric tingles shooting through my upper back.

I felt like I had been hit by a freight train. My hands were completely numb and so was my entire face. I barely managed to lift the face shield and remove my headset cap. It was of no use anymore without a communication system to be connected to. The ringing in my ears had stopped, replaced by a faint sound like TV static in the background. I tilted my head ever so slightly and realized it was the sound of my parachute rustling in the wind.

I looked around. The lake was nowhere in sight, and neither were Max or any of the other racers. Right before my eyes had been forced shut by the ejection, I caught a glimpse of Max's plane diving vertically toward the side of the mountain. He must have crashed, but there were no signs around me that he had. No debris, nothing.

The events of the last few days flashed through my mind: Central City, the nationals, Julianne, Max, Vinnie, Dr.

Allen, the flight controls I'd been gripping not too long before. Literally every part of my body ached.

I drifted toward the ground like an autumn leaf falling from a tree. There were several fields below me; some seemed to be planted in parallel rows, and others had what looked like small bushes among the rows. It looked like I wouldn't be landing in the middle of the desert. I felt a sense of relief knowing that there would likely be someone around given that it looked like farmlands. My throat was really hurting. It must have been from all the cold air I had swallowed.

As I got closer to the ground, I crossed my fingers that I wouldn't land in one of the bushes. They looked awfully prickly. Then I laughed at myself. What difference would a few scratches and cuts make after being shot out of a plane with the force of twelve times Earth's gravity? It was life over limb, just like they said in training camp.

Reaching the ground, I attempted to unstrap myself from the ejection seat assembly but my hands were too numb to work the latches. The moment my feet touched the ground, I collapsed backward, my legs as unresponsive as a pair of cinderblocks.

CHAPTER 13

I reached for the crash kit under the seat, a yellow plastic box with the NJRA logo on it. I dumped the contents onto the ground in front of me and scrambled through them for the survival knife. I unfolded the survival knife and slipped the blade under the harness, remembering from training camp to cut away from myself rather than toward my body. The thick material of the strap resisted as I sawed at it with the serrated edge; black dust fibres covered my hand.

The shimmer from the lake in the distance caught my eye as I crawled off the seat, finally free. I couldn't tell how far it was to the lake, but a surge of energy rushed through me as I eased myself to my feet, my body no longer feeling like concrete. But I was uneasy, even though there was nobody else in sight.

I stuffed the pockets of my flight jacket with supplies from the crash kit: emergency food rations, water purification tablets, and a stainless-steel water bottle. I grabbed the radio beacon and switched it on.

I didn't know how long it would be until they found me, but I figured if I moved closer to the lake, they'd find me sooner.

"Hello, is anyone around?" I shouted.

Oh shit, what have I done?

I picked up the knife and held it in front of me, looking around in case Max showed up. That tiny three-inch folding knife would be pretty useless against someone like him, but it was better than nothing.

The lake seemed far away, perhaps too far to walk to, but I heard babbling water closer by and decided to follow the sound. I limped toward it, but within minutes my body began to ache again.

Finally, I arrived at the edge of a stream. I sat down on a flat rock beside it and put the knife down within reach. I dunked the water bottle into the stream before dropping a purification tablet into it. The tablet made a fizzing sound as it hit the water. As I took a big gulp of purified stream water, I was brought back to the time when I drank the wine at my first communion with my adoptive parents. My hands began to shake as I reached to refill the bottle from the stream. It fell in and was washed away with the current.

I reached for my phone in my pocket to see if there was any signal. I wanted to text Mike to let him know that I had landed safely. My back was aching so badly that it was hard to sit upright, let alone reach into my pocket. My eyelids felt as heavy as anvils as I slumped backward onto the flat rock. My head was spinning and I shut my eyes.

I heard a man with a deep voice speak into a radio. "Rescue Boat Two to NJRA. He has been located and recovered. We are now on our way back."

"Copy that," another voice replied.

I struggled to turn my head, but managed to have a look around me. I was on a rescue boat, lying on what looked like a hospital stretcher, the kind with wheels they use to push people around the wards. I was hooked up to a monitor that displayed my heart rate, body temperature, breathing rate, oxygen levels, and blood pressure on a black screen. I could feel a block of some sort under my legs.

"Jay Smith, how're you feeling?" the medic who'd spoken on the radio asked me. "Can you remember what happened?"

"Last I remember, I was sitting on a rock next to a stream," I mumbled.

"You passed out near the stream, not too far from the lake."

"At least I didn't land *in* the water."

"How's the pain on a scale of one to ten?" he asked as he scribbled some notes on a notepad.

"About seven or eight. I've got a migraine."

He nodded.

"Does everyone at the stadium know I'm okay?" I asked.

"We've notified the stadium via radio. Your league mates should get the message soon enough."

I could only imagine how worried Mike and the others must be.

"You actually came out pretty well from it," The medic remarked. "No broken bones. As far as we can tell, nothing more than two dislocated fingers on your right hand and the whiplash you've described. Mathias wasn't in such good shape when we found him after he ejected; the leg restraints broke both his legs."

"At least I didn't break my neck like Mike did when he ejected years ago."

"In all my years in this job, it's not often we see cases like this," the medic said, smiling.

All of the fingers on my right hand had been taped together to prevent further dislocation, just like they had taught us for first aid in ground school. An ice pack was placed under that hand.

"I don't even remember my hand hurting until the parachute opened," I said. "It must have been from gripping the ejection handle right as the rocket motors were activated."

"It's the adrenaline. I tell you, it's your body's natural painkiller."

The ice pack was also doing a good job of numbing the pain, since most of the adrenaline had long worn off.

"Apparently it wasn't enough to stop me from passing out."

"Ejecting puts a whole lot of stress on your body," he explained. "But you should be glad those seats have come a long way since the old days. It saved your life."

"Guess my back's going to be sore for a while," I said, remembering how one ejection had left Mike with a lifetime of pain. *I can't imagine how Mike manages to push the breakfast cart around and take out the trash when he feels like this every day.*

"You'll learn to live with it," he replied.

"You're still young, so you'll heal pretty well." He put a blanket on me. "We'll be back at the stadium in about twenty minutes, so I suggest you get some rest. You're probably exhausted."

"Aren't we going to the hospital?"

"The air ambulance is waiting at the dock near the stadium," he replied.

"My plane's totalled, isn't it?" I asked. I didn't even want to think about how much would come out of my paycheque for that.

"Pretty much."

A couple tears fell from my eyes as I grieved for #80. There was no doubt I was exhausted, but images of my plane in pieces at the scrapyard filled my mind, keeping me awake. I lifted my left arm to take a look at my nails, still painted phoenix-orange.

The boat docked. I must have actually fallen asleep for some part of those twenty minutes, as they went by much faster than I'd expected. A red and white helicopter was waiting as I was taken off the boat. I was transferred onto a different stretcher and, once I was on the helicopter, I was hooked up to similar monitors. The medic from the boat handed me my flight jacket and boots before the helicopter door was closed.

This stretcher wasn't as comfortable as the one on the boat. I felt my heart pounding as the helicopter lifted off. The feeling of flying again had me panicking, and it didn't help that I was right next to a window. The helicopter hovered for a few seconds and then continued ascending. A female attendant with curly brown hair was sitting across from me on the left.

"How's the pain on a scale of one to ten?" she asked. "One being nothing, ten being the absolute worst pain you've ever felt."

"Seven," I replied. I felt like it had gone down a little from when the boat medic had asked that question. Maybe chatting with him just as the adrenaline was wearing off had distracted me from the pain. "Feels like when you work out too hard and it hurts, not to mention my head feels like it's about to split open."

"Can you lift your arms and wiggle your legs for me?"

I lifted both my arms up and wiggled my feet. My arms still felt a bit heavy.

"Looks good. I like your nails by the way," she said in a way that reminded me of Dr. Allen when he did my evaluation.

I blushed. She must have noticed them when I was lifting my arms.

"Didn't get a chance to do my other hand," I replied.

"My nine-year-old loves painting her nails too, but sometimes she asks me to help her because she tends to make a mess all over her fingers."

"By the way, will I be able to walk again?"

"From the look of things, definitely," she said with a smile. "But in accordance with NJRA protocol, we still have to take you to the hospital to be checked out. They're probably going to take some X-rays. Is there anything else you think they should know about? Changes in vision, hearing, numbness in the arms or legs?"

"There's a high-pitched ringing in my ears that fades in and out."

"That's tinnitus from acoustic trauma, which is just a fancy term for ringing in the ears after a loud noise. You probably know how ejection seats work with rocket motors and explosives, and while those systems are great, the amount of noise is an unfortunate side effect. It's like putting your ear next to a jet engine as it's taking off," she explained.

"Does it go away?"

"I can't say exactly, as it's different for everyone, but I'm sure the doctor can offer a better opinion on that."

I decided to lay back and try to rest a bit more until we arrived at the hospital. It was only then that I noticed the warmth from the sunlight streaming through the window. It was surprisingly quiet inside the helicopter, or maybe it was from the hearing damage.

I watched as the helicopter descended toward the roof of the hospital. After my stretcher had been wheeled off, I stood up with a bit of support from the attendant. It wasn't exactly painful, but my legs shook. I didn't think I'd be able to take more than a few steps without losing my balance. I sat down in a hospital wheelchair. A ward attendant wheeled me into an elevator that must've been big enough to fit several of those chairs and he pushed the button for the ground floor.

I watched the numbers on the LED display go down, taking care not to tilt my head back too much. It must have taken almost five minutes to reach the ground floor with all the stops the elevator made on the way, other wheelchairs and medical equipment being pushed in and out.

As I was wheeled past the waiting area of the emergency room, several people were staring at a TV in the corner. The news channel was on. A male news anchor was on the screen with the words 'Breaking News' in bold white letters above him. I couldn't hear the TV over the ringing in my ears, but I could read the subtitles.

"Chaos has erupted at Westcoast Airsports Stadium as this year's NJRA Nationals came to a bloody end with two racers dead in two days," the anchor said. "Kiera Lam has the story."

The ward attendant stopped to talk with one of the nurses behind the desk as I continued to watch the news report.

"Thanks, Robin. Fights are breaking out in the grandstands, and food, drinks, binoculars, and shoes are being thrown at racers' jets by enraged spectators. Ash Christie has been tackled by an angry fan who charged at him as he walked out onto the runway."

A nurse sitting behind the desk stood up. He wheeled me into an exam room before I had a chance to see what was happening to Ash. He helped me stand up from the wheelchair and get onto the exam table.

"You'll be seeing Dr. King. She'll be here shortly," he said. He shut the door on his way out.

There was a knock on the door several minutes later.

"Hello, Jayson. I'm Dr. King." A woman in blue scrubs with her hair in a ponytail came into the room. As much as I hated being called Jayson, I couldn't be bothered to tell her. "So, it looks like they were monitoring your vitals on the way here and everything seems good. Can you tell me more about your pain?"

"My neck's killing me. I must've snapped my head back right when I ejected."

"I see. Your eyes are quite swollen. Are you seeing any spots of light, blurriness, or anything like that?"

I lifted my left hand up to my left eye. I could definitely feel that the skin around my eye was puffy. I felt my other eye. It was about the same.

"My vision was a bit blurry as I was parachuting down, but by the time I was in the rescue boat, it was fine."

"That's good to hear. It doesn't seem like anything too serious, and the swelling usually goes down by itself. Let's have a look at your neck."

She put her clipboard down on the counter next to her and put on some plastic gloves. She moved her fingers around my neck, feeling every bone closely.

"Tell me if it hurts."

"Yeah, right there," I said. It was in the back, halfway down my neck on both sides.

"Is it a sharp, shooting pain, or more of a dull ache?"

"It's more a tight pain."

"Is there any numbness or an electricity-like sensation that moves through your arms or down your back when you try to turn your head?"

"There was a bit earlier, but now it just feels really stiff."

"Alright. It looks like your neck is fine from a bone perspective, but I'll order an X-ray just to be sure as well as a

CT scan of your head. I'm going to have a look at your right hand now if that's okay."

She lifted the ice pack off my hand and placed it on the counter next to her clipboard. Then, she peeled off the tape that was wrapped around my fingers. It was the first time I had seen my own fingers since I had ejected. They were bruised, swollen, and looked slightly misshapen.

"Your index and middle fingers are definitely dislocated. They'll need to be realigned, so I'm going to do that next. You'll get a couple shots to numb the area first."

I began shaking. I've always hated needles and dreaded my physicals because of the blood tests that were required. I was that kid who would run out of the doctor's office and down the hallway screaming my head off every time I had to get a shot.

"You're not scared to fly planes but you're scared of needles?"

I had no response to that.

She left the room for a couple minutes. I tried not to think about shots or the urge that came from deep down to run screaming out of the room like I used to, even though I knew I would probably stumble and fall on my face, given my shaky legs.

"Look away if it's easier," she said, wiping down my fingers with alcohol.

I stared at a poster on the wall to distract myself. It was a diagram of all the nerves in the human body. The shots weren't too bad, not comfortable, but not as bad as I'd expected. It was more of a burning feeling than anything else.

"Do you feel anything now?" she asked, touching my hand and pushing on my index finger.

"Nothing at all," I answered. It was like my right hand wasn't even attached to my body, even though I could see it right in front of me and I could still move it, except for the two dislocated fingers.

"Ready now?"

I nodded. She started with my index finger. I watched her pull on it, but there was no pain. I felt just a bit of a pressure in my arm.

"That one's all done. I'll do the other one and then we'll get you in for an X-ray and a CT."

The other finger seemed even easier than the first.

"That wasn't too bad, was it? Can you move your fingers?"

It felt weird to be able to move my fingers again. She put a new ice pack on my hand, picked up her clipboard, and left the room. The same nurse came in and wheeled me to the X-ray department. The technician first took X-rays of my neck including a left view, a right view, and a back view, and then one of my right hand. Next I was wheeled into the waiting area for a CT scan.

After I was taken back to the exam room, I thought about texting Mike to let him know where I was. I held my phone on my lap with the palm of my right hand and used my left hand to type. I asked Mike if he was alright and if he had managed to escape the chaos at the stadium. Then I texted Vinnie with the same question. There was no reply from either of them.

As I waited, I noticed that my legs were feeling much less heavy and sore. Holding on to the exam table for balance, I stood up from the wheelchair. I tried walking a few steps to the chair next to the counter. I was so relieved that my shaky legs had calmed down enough for me to stand and even walk on them that I spent the next several minutes trying to walk around the room. I didn't lose my balance even once. Finally I sat down in the chair next to the counter.

The door opened and Dr. King walked in. She didn't seem too surprised to see me sitting in the chair instead of the wheelchair. She sat in a chair opposite me.

"Jayson, I've had a look at your X-rays and CT scan. Your neck and upper back are fine, but X-rays can't show muscle injuries. The tightness and pain you're describing is definitely a whiplash injury, and part of it could be related to stress too, given your situation. How are your legs feeling now?"

"I can stand up and walk now," I replied, smiling.

"If you don't mind, could you take a few steps for me?"

I stood up, bracing myself with one hand on the wall in case I lost my balance. I took a few steps toward her, and then turned and walked back to the chair.

"Wonderful. I guess you won't need the wheelchair anymore. I'll be sending the records to your primary doctor who should call you in a week or so for follow-up. In the meantime, take it easy, avoid lifting anything heavy, and be careful not to twist your neck when you're sleeping. For the pain and swelling, take Advil Extra Strength three times a day and see how you feel. I don't think any further care is needed from our side, so I'm going to have you sign right here for me."

She handed me her clipboard and pen and pointed at the line on the bottom of the patient discharge form. I signed the form and handed it back.

"It was nice meeting you, Jayson, and I wish you a safe trip home. I'll walk with you out to the waiting room. Do you have someone picking you up?"

"I think so," I replied, taking my phone out of my pocket with my left hand. "Just have to text him."

"If you have any concerns, one of the nurses will be able to help you," she said. "Other than that, all the best."

I sat down in a chair across from the TV and texted Mike. The TV was still turned to the news channel. My ears continued ringing, so I ended up reading the subtitles again.

"The crowds have now been dispersed by stadium security who had to protect racers, pit crew, and other stadium staff after chaos erupted this afternoon at Westcoast Airsports Stadium following the death of racer Max Erikson during round three of the NJRA Nationals. Here we have a recap of the events from earlier this afternoon."

The newscast cut to a scene of paper plates, partially eaten food, shoes, and various other items being hurled at the runway as the racers were landing their planes. The camera zoomed in on Ash climbing out of his cockpit.

"Here we see Wyoming's Ash Christie being tackled and thrown to the ground by an angry spectator who had rushed out of the grandstands and onto the runway."

The video went into slow motion and zoomed in even

closer on the spectator grabbing the front of Ash's flight jacket and attempting to throw him face first onto the tarmac. I wanted to look away, but I just could not take my eyes off the scene. *That must be how everyone in the grandstands was feeling when Julianne's crash was playing on the Jumbotron over and over.*

My phone rang, taking my attention away from the TV. It was Mike.

"Hey, Jay, I got your message that you're leaving the hospital and everything's alright. They're sending a shuttle bus for you. How are you feeling?"

His voice sounded strained as he wheezed slightly between sentences.

"Pretty devastated. Is everything okay?" I asked.

"Just caught a bit of pepper spray earlier." He coughed.

"Was the whole stadium trashed?"

"Nope, just the stands, the runway, and some of the hangar area. The racers' building is fine. Thank God that angry mob didn't get nowhere near there."

"So it's safe to go back?" I asked.

"Yeah. It was pretty crazy a few hours ago, but the crowds are all cleared out now."

"Do you know if Ash is okay?"

"Just a black eye from having a shoe thrown at him."

"I thought he got tackled. Wasn't he hurt?"

"They roughed him up a bit, but I ran up there and managed to shove the guy off him with my cane," Mike replied.

I couldn't believe it. A guy like him who walked with a limp and spent practically every day in pain rushing onto the scene to keep a fellow jet racer from being hurt by an angry spectator.

"You could've been hurt or something."

"There're seven hundred security guards looking after fifty thousand people. I wasn't going to just stand around and wait. Anyways, I got a few things to take care of now. Talk to you later."

My phone rang again; this time it was my adoptive mom.

"Hi, Jay. Your dad and I just saw what happened on TV. Are you at the hospital?"

"Yeah, though I've just been discharged."

"Is someone picking you up?"

"Yeah, the league's sent a shuttle bus for me."

"I guess you weren't too badly hurt, then. It looked pretty intense up there."

"No broken bones, just two dislocated fingers. Though my neck really hurts; whiplash, the doctor says."

"Oh, thank God. You must've snapped your neck back pretty hard when you were shot out of that plane."

"Sure did," I replied. The ringing in my ears had gotten louder, making it harder to hear what she was saying. "I feel like I've been hit by a freight train and I'm going to be in pain for the rest of my life now."

"Your dad and I will be praying for you. You just have to believe and you will feel better. Open that Bible I gave you before you left."

THE JET RACER

There she goes again. I still couldn't believe that she'd insisted on giving me a Bible even though I had stopped going to church almost two years before leaving for training camp.

I just said a quick "Bye" and hung up on her.

The shuttle bus arrived, though it was actually a passenger van, not a full-size bus. There was no shortage of "Go, Max, Go" and Team Max signs in the windows of sports bars and cars as we drove through the city. There were a few Team Jay signs too, but it wasn't hard to see who the majority of that town had been rooting for.

The shuttle drove around the stadium grounds, giving me a good view of the kind of damage the crowd had done. The jumbotron across from the empty grandstands was covered in cracks and scratches. Paper plates, cups, and bits of food littered the ground around the stands, runway, and pit area. Stadium staff walked around the grandstands with mops, brooms, and dustpans.

They sure trashed the place. I couldn't believe how seriously people took the sport, treating its participants like gods. *How can I be a part of this ridiculous circus anymore?*

The shuttle parked in front of the racers' building. The stench of stale beer hit me in the face as I opened the door.

Mike was waiting for me. His face was still red from the pepper spray.

"Good to see you're alright," he said, walking with me to the building.

"I'm done for," I sighed.

"Hey, I'm done for too," he said. "Ain't working for the NJRA no more. I've been canned."

"What for?"

"The whole thing with Julianne."

"Really? But it's not your fault."

"As the league caretaker, it's my job to make sure the planes are working the way they should be," he replied. "And now that something's gone wrong, it's all chalked up to me."

He stopped and faced me.

"Listen, Jay, you've probably heard this already, but rest as much as you can. Ejecting's very hard on the body."

"I will," I replied. "I feel like my whole body's made of concrete."

"Remind me to give you some of the arnica cream I use on my back. It's a lifesaver."

I felt my neck ache as I nodded.

"In case I don't see you later tonight, there's a charter plane picking you and me up tomorrow morning. It's leaving at nine sharp to take us back to the airfield."

CHAPTER 14

I tapped my key card to enter the racers' building. Mike was right; the angry mobs had left that part of the stadium alone. I went to the men's sleeping quarters and grabbed a change of clothes from my suitcase. After a quick shower, I made my way down to the dining hall. A slideshow of photos of Julianne and Max throughout their NJRA careers was being projected on a screen in the corner. I couldn't look at it for even one minute without tearing up. I decided to have dinner alone.

I still smell like jet fuel, I thought as I got up from the table. The odour was giving me a headache.

Irene was standing at the end of the hallway, in front of the bathrooms, chatting with Ash. He was carrying a towel and his hair was all wet. I had seen Irene in the dining hall earlier, but I didn't talk to her then.

"Jay, glad you're okay," she said. "I was really worried about you."

"I hope you never have to eject," I replied. "I was lucky enough not to break any bones."

"I can imagine. Your neck looks like it hurts, though."

"I've got a migraine too, so I'm going back to the sleeping quarters to get some rest," I said, rubbing my forehead. "Any idea on Andrew's whereabouts? I haven't seen him since yesterday."

"They sent him back home," she replied. "He's suspended from NJRA functions until further notice."

"Like home as in back to Boston?"

She nodded. "He's under investigation for accusations of cheating and sabotage."

My jaw dropped.

"Cheating?" Ash asked, raising his eyebrows. "Why the hell would someone sabotage their own engine to make it fail?"

"It's not *his* plane that he's suspected of sabotaging," she explained. She hesitated. "It was Julianne's."

Her voice was a mix of anger and grief as she said that name.

So he's the culprit, then.

"Maybe he was so angry about what happened in the first round," I said. Maybe Andrew just wanted to take it out on someone. I knew how that felt, but I'd never acted on it.

"Hey guys, what's up?" Russ said, stepping out of the men's bathroom.

"We were just talking about the fact that they sent Andrew home," Irene said.

"They tried to blame it on the pit guys, especially Gerry. He was the one who forgot to put away that can of WD-40," Russ said. "I heard he ended up with a warning from the NJRA, and he'll have to pay for the can that was sprayed in your face by you-know-who."

"So they found proof that Andrew did it and that the can of WD-40 was involved?" I asked.

"They found a whole set of metal files from the pit area in his suitcase," Irene said. "Mike said that Andrew's key card was found on the hangar floor yesterday morning, so he probably dropped it when he was digging through the toolboxes."

"Then why was the WD-40 found next to your plane?" Russ asked, looking at me.

"Because Andrew planted it there," Irene replied, "so everyone would blame it on Jay."

Everything made sense at that point, but it seemed too extreme that Mike was getting blamed because he failed to notice that Julianne's plane had been tampered with before the race. Would Andrew only get a slap on the wrist because the NJRA cared more about him than about Mike? After all, Mike was just an old man with a cane who hadn't been famous for years. There was also the fact that Andrew was the son of a retired racer and had it easier because he never had to grow up on food stamps.

"Sorry, guys, but I have to go," I said, stepping away from the three of them.

The memories of Julianne flooded my mind as I stood outside the men's sleeping quarters. I glanced over at the doorway of the women's sleeping quarters, wanting to look through Julianne's suitcase again. I poked my head through the doorway. The lights were off and there was not a single person inside. If anyone walked by and asked what I was doing in there, I'd say I was looking for Irene. There was a feeling of melancholy as I stepped inside, seeing three beds with suitcases underneath, Sara's, Irene's, and Julianne's, and knowing that only two of them were being used.

I kept turning to look behind me as I walked over to Julianne's bed. My neck ached with every turn and my head throbbed. Her pillow was still wrinkled from when she had last slept on it. The covers were crumpled at the foot of the bed. I pulled her suitcase out from under the bed. The zipper was open. I grabbed the first article of clothing from the top of it. It was a dress made from a solid black, silky material. I had only ever seen her wear it once. I could feel my heart racing as I rolled up the dress so that nobody could tell what it was if they saw me holding it. Then I looked both ways down the hall before leaving the room.

I returned to the men's sleeping quarters. The Bruce Dickinson book was still next to my pillow where I had left it. I guessed it was mine to keep, as was the black dress. Joe was sitting on his bed and typing on his laptop. He didn't even seem to notice me in the room as he was so focused on what he was doing. I stuffed the dress into my suitcase.

I climbed onto my bed and picked up the book. As I flipped it open, Max Erikson's name, written in blue ink on the lower right corner of the first page caught my eye. My throat tightened as I glanced at those ten letters. I shut the book and tossed it onto Vinnie's bed. Joe looked at me for a second before turning back to his laptop. I leaned over the edge of my bed and grabbed a T-shirt from my suitcase, then lay down for a nap, covering my eyes with the shirt, hoping to sleep off that migraine.

The T-shirt fell off my face after what seemed like an hour. My head was no longer throbbing, but the entire room seemed to move as I sat up on my bed. Vertigo. Joe had left and there was nobody else in the room.

After the vertigo had passed, I took Julianne's makeup bag out of my suitcase and unzipped it. A tube of eyeliner caught my eye. I held it in my hand for a moment. There were silver stars etched all over the tube, and the seal of crinkly plastic wrap had yet to be broken. It must have been quite expensive, just like the rest of her makeup. I began to imagine myself as Julianne, wearing a flowy, casual dress and walking into the makeup department of a high-end department store in New York City during the off-season. A salesperson would hand me a little shopping basket and I would spend hours browsing through all the different brands and colours, before picking out my favourites and placing them in the basket.

The thought of the black dress kept popping into my mind. I imagined how it would look on me, but I realized I didn't have any shoes to wear with it.

My train of thought was interrupted by a knock at the door. A man wearing a white dress shirt and black pants stood in the doorway. A silver name tag, like Dr. Allen's, was pinned to his shirt, though I couldn't read it from where I sat.

"Good evening," he said. "My name's Aaron McNeill. I'm the manager of members' services for the NJRA." He had that familiar air of coldness and robotic tone of voice that all the other officials had.

Not another meeting with an official.

I got up off my bed and followed him to the same office where Dr. Allen and the health and safety officials had interrogated me. He turned on the lights and sat down behind the desk.

"As you are aware, the NJRA's policies state that once a pilot has experienced an ejection, they are no longer fit to fly for the association."

I nodded, feeling a lump in my throat. This is what had happened to Mike years ago.

"It may seem unfair, but these policies are for your safety. Ejection is very hard on the body, as you now know, and unfortunately you're deemed unfit to fly because of it," Aaron explained.

I nodded.

"At least we can be grateful that you weren't seriously hurt," he said.

There he was, pretending to sound like he truly cared about me while talking to me like I was just another number.

"But if I can still walk, see, and hear fine, for the most part, how come I can't fly?" I asked.

"Medical issues can arise years after ejection. The NJRA would rather be safe than sorry. Have you heard about Michael Collins, the astronaut?"

"No, I haven't." I never paid much attention in science class, nor could I remember ever hearing that name.

"Before he was an astronaut, he was a test pilot for the US Air Force. He was once forced to eject from an F-86 after an engine fire. Ten years later, he started having problems with his back and legs that were traced back to the ejection," he explained in that flat, monotonous voice.

It was a hard truth for me to swallow. It seemed like only yesterday that I was accepted into the NJRA's training camp a couple months before my eighteenth birthday. And now it was ending like this. Even dying in a fiery crash seemed like it would be better. At least it would be painless, because the heat would knock you out before you boiled from the inside out, according to my old science teacher.

I cleared my throat. "I understand."

"Now, try not to get too upset. You have plenty of other options for staying with the NJRA."

It wasn't hard to figure out that doing Mike's job was one of those options. I tried to imagine myself as a league caretaker, but I just could not see myself giving quality flying advice to rookies the way Mike had done for me over the past two years.

"There are plenty of jobs with the NJRA that don't involve flying, but your flight experience can be an asset," he explained. "How do you feel about working in the pits?"

"I thought pit crew members were just people who graduated from training camp but didn't get into a league." At least that's what everyone says.

"Some of them are, but some are former pilots like you. Not all pilots quit because they can't fly anymore. Some of them burn out from racing; others just decide it's no longer for them. But they still love being around planes, so they work in the pit."

I had nothing to say about that.

"Think about it. Whatever job you choose, you'll have

to stick with it for one season. Then, if you don't like it, you can change your mind and try something else."

I nodded.

"Or maybe you'd be interested in becoming a league caretaker."

I just could not see myself doing Mike's job because of all the responsibilities that came with it. And after the excitement of flying, washing planes and picking up mail would get boring pretty fast, just like working in the pits.

"If you don't mind working at a desk, there are options for that as well."

"Will I have to move to another town?" I asked, trying to pretend I was interested in any of those jobs when deep down I knew I wasn't.

"Only if you want to."

I applied to training camp because I wanted to fly. I would never forget the excitement of flying a plane for the first time. It was like I'd been born to do it. And then I'd gained a fan following in just one season for being the youngest pilot in the nationals. There wasn't any point in working for the NJRA if I didn't get to fly. I was a bird who'd had its wings clipped—quite literally—by Max.

"I'm just wondering." I paused, gulping. "What if I was to quit the NJRA?"

"Are you sure none of these jobs appeal to you?" he asked. "Is there anything you like to do outside of flying?"

"I like listening to music."

"What about becoming a sound technician at the races? That might be a good choice."

"But I don't really know anything about music. I can't even play an instrument."

"You can apply for an NJRA grant to attend a sound engineering program. Some programs don't even require you to know music theory or how to play an instrument."

"Can't you just tell me what would happen if I was to leave the NJRA?"

"I don't recommend it." His voice told me that he was grasping at straws to get me to stay. "But since you asked, here are the regulations that relate to terminating your contract."

From his briefcase, he pulled out a thick stack of paper that was held together with a large staple and flipped it open. It was then that I realized that there was more to leaving than just packing up and going home to wherever home was for you.

"First, you would have to turn in your plane, but since yours is totalled, that doesn't apply to you."

"But I still have to pay for it, right?" I asked, even though I knew the answer was likely yes.

"I'll get to that. Your NJRA-specific type rating would be revoked, but you would still be able to keep a private pilot's licence."

"So I'm still allowed to fly?"

"Only personal aircraft less than twelve and a half thousand pounds and not equipped with an ejection seat. If you did continue flying, you would still have to undergo the same medical exam every year. Also, if you pursued an aviation career outside the NJRA, you could put that you've completed your PPL on your résumé. There are plenty of jobs in the field that don't involve flying, but that will be up to you to decide."

I took a deep breath.

"You would forfeit your NJRA accommodation privileges, which include your airfield privileges as well as your apartment," he continued.

"So that means I'll have to find my own place?"

The thought of returning to my adoptive parents' house didn't appeal to me, especially since I had been away for so long.

He nodded. "We would no longer be able to help you in any way once you have decided to break your contract. Which brings me to the next part."

He flipped ahead several pages and pointed his finger at a paragraph almost halfway down the page.

He began reading. "Once your contract has been terminated, you are no longer allowed to have any direct communication with active NJRA members, including racers, pit crew, flight instructors, administration staff, or any immediate family of active members. Contractors providing temporary services at venues where NJRA events are held are not included. Direct communication includes, but is not limited to, email, letter mail, text messages, phone calls, and social media connections."

No one had told me this when I signed my contract with the NJRA. It meant I would never hear from Vinnie or Irene, or any of the others for that matter. On one hand, I was so done with NJRA life, but on the other hand, I couldn't imagine leaving my friends behind.

"Will I still be allowed to attend races?"

"You could still purchase tickets to NJRA events as a member of the general public, but you would not be allowed to have any direct contact with any active members present, nor would you be allowed into areas that are restricted to active members only."

At least I'd have a chance of seeing Vinnie and Irene and everyone else, although it would be like I didn't exist to them, almost like I was a ghost, watching the race and knowing many of the racers up in the sky. I would see Vinnie's face behind the canopy of his blue #37 as he sped down the runway and I would wave at him from the stands. Except my hand would be one of thousands in the crowd, like a single raindrop in a puddle. All the memories of that one season I spent with him would drown me like a flood, just like the memories of Julianne.

"Uh, I have another question," I said, feeling the words stuck in my throat. "Am I allowed to attend Max and Julianne's memorial service at the league airfield if I end my contract today?"

"We would allow you to stay at the airfield until the memorial service. Your league would arrange for a shuttle bus to pick you up the day after with all your belongings."

"If my apartment is gone, then where will the shuttle take me?"

My adoptive parents wouldn't be expecting me. I would have to give them a call and then show up on their doorstep.

"It would still take you back to your apartment at the NJRA off-season housing complex. There's a one-month grace period from the day you terminate the contract before your accommodation privileges are revoked. That would give you some time to sort things out," he explained. He flipped several pages ahead in the booklet. "This brings me to the final part, the financial matters. For terminating your contract, there would be an initial debt of nine hundred thousand dollars, which you would have to pay off in increments overtime."

"What?" I felt my jaw drop.

"A financial advisor would be in touch with you within a week or so to discuss further details."

"Is there anything else? Like hidden fees?"

"Yes. The initial amount is to repay the expense of your training and accommodations, both on-season and off-season. Additional amounts would cover expenses such as aircraft maintenance, facilities maintenance, and medical expenses."

Instead of taking the cost of my totalled plane out of my paycheque, they'd add it to my debt. After all, I was no longer going to have a paycheque for them to take it out of.

"So what happens when someone retires from the NJRA, then? Do they have to pay back all that?"

"Retirement is a different story. Active members may retire at the age of sixty with full benefits. Race pilots may apply for retirement at the age of forty, and are required to retire once they reach forty-five, at which time they have the option to take full benefits or to switch to a non-flying position."

He turned to the last page of the booklet. At the bottom was a signature line. He picked up the pen and handed it to me.

"I've offered you several options and explained the consequences of termination. You can sign this now, but you have seven days to decide. I advise you to take the time to think it over carefully."

"I've made up my mind," I replied with confidence. I was disgusted just thinking about how Andrew's family would likely pay off the NJRA to not ban him for life. How Julianne had been treated like a piece of meat. How Irene was put on a pedestal for being openly lesbian. How Max had gotten barely a slap on the wrist for assault.

"Are you sure?"

I hesitated for a moment before touching the tip of the pen to the page. My hands began shaking and I paused halfway through my signature, knowing I could still back out. I finished my signature and handed the pen to him. He signed above the witness line without a second thought. He then put a stamp in the empty spot between both of our signatures. The stamp was the NJRA logo with the date below it.

"Thank you, Jayson. I wish you all the best in whatever future endeavours you choose to pursue." He stood up and shook my hand.

I left the office and walked quickly back to the sleeping quarters, not wanting to look at anyone along the way. I picked up the Bruce Dickinson book from Vinnie's bed and stuffed it into my suitcase. I'd give it to him personally when I broke the news that I was leaving the NJRA. I stared at

Vinnie's bed for a moment, wiping my tears on my sleeve as I sobbed.

I picked up my toiletries kit and went down the hallway to the bathroom. Looking at myself in the mirror as I brushed my teeth, I noticed how long my hair had gotten. It was starting to look a bit messy, but I wanted to keep growing it out. It wasn't hard to imagine how much work Julianne put into making her long hair look so nice all the time.

I thought about seeing if Irene was in the women's sleeping quarters so I could break the news to her. Then I decided that I might as well tell her and Vinnie at the same time.

It was hard to believe that only a day ago, I'd been sitting next to him watching a science documentary. It was only a day ago that I had painted my nails phoenix-orange. I could not bear to even look at them anymore. I wondered if there was any nail polish remover in Julianne's makeup bag.

CHAPTER 15

The charter plane was waiting for me on the runway after breakfast. Taking one last look at the hangars that housed the planes at the stadium, I reflected on what they represented: all the friendships I had made over the last two years. Now they were no longer part of my life. I would never see life the same way again.

"C'mon, Jay, we're leaving," Mike shouted from the top step of the plane's stairs.

I wanted to ask what the results of the last race had been, but I realized he probably had a lot on his mind already. After all, now that he had to leave the NJRA, he was likely facing the same sort of debts that I was, even though he was being kicked out as opposed to choosing to break his contract.

I took my seat in the first row next to Mike. As I looked out the window at the stadium hangars again, my eyes teared up.

"I guess you know how it feels to be done for good now," I said.

"I can't believe it's been seven years already," he

replied. "Maybe it's for the best, after all. My back could really use a change."

"Heading home to Dallas? I bet you miss it."

"Yeah, for now. Then I'll see where life takes me next. Hopefully I'll find a girl to spend my life with."

"I mean, it's not really your fault. It's unfortunate that the NJRA is putting the blame on you for what happened."

"It's the way things are," he replied. "Just have to play the hand you're dealt."

"I wanted to say thanks for all the tips and whatnot you gave me for flying in the nationals." I shook his hand. "As well as all the work you did for us at the airfield. You took good care of the place and everyone's planes."

"Just doing my job," he smiled, leaning over to put his cane under the seat. "But now that my back's starting to get the best of me, it's better I don't do this kind of work anyway."

When he mentioned his own pain, I became aware of the ache still lingering in my back.

"I don't know if I can last another season," Mike added. "It's a struggle to even walk some days."

"Yikes, that's hard. I hope it doesn't get that bad for me."

"It made me happy just to be able to help others," he explained. "But now, even that's over."

"Actually, Mike, I have something to tell you," I stuttered a bit as I said this.

Mike's fatherly eyes gazed back at me.

"I've, um, left the NJRA. They're giving me a month's

time to move out of my apartment, but I'm not a member anymore."

Mike looked surprised. Then he said, "Remember, I was in your spot years ago. I know it feels like the end of the world, because it did for me when I had to stop flying. But that doesn't mean you have to leave."

No amount of convincing was going to change anything for me. The decision was made, and the papers were signed.

"But you still wanted to stay in the NJRA?" I asked.

"You see," Mike explained, "if I had left, I would have been leaving my health insurance too. The healthcare system couldn't care less about people in pain, because they think it ain't serious. And besides, I made so much more as a league caretaker than I would have on welfare."

His words reminded me that my pain could last for years too, even though my injuries were much less severe than his had been.

"I think I want to go back to school, you know, finish high school," I said. "At least that would open up more opportunities for me when it comes to looking for work."

"You've learned more in the NJRA than you ever will in school. Trust me on that."

My mind wandered to the Bruce Dickinson book in my suitcase. I definitely didn't want to take it with me after I left my racing career behind. In fact, I never wanted to see that book again or have anything to do with it, whether it had Max Erikson's name written on it or not.

The charter plane landed at Central City Jet Racing

League Airfield an hour later. I walked down the steps and through the empty hangar, where there was nothing left of my plane or Julianne's, Andrew's, or Max's, except for a few drops of engine oil on the hangar floor where they once stood. There was a general feeling of emptiness inside me as I walked through the airfield hangar. That same feeling of emptiness and melancholy filled my body as I passed the open door of Julianne's dorm room on the way to mine.

I took the Bruce Dickinson book with me as I went to the lunchroom to look for Vinnie.

The rumble of jet engines outside interrupted the silence. Vinnie and Irene must have just gotten back from the stadium. Several minutes later, I heard Vinnie's voice from the lunchroom doorway.

"Jay, glad you're okay!" His whole face lit up as he hurried toward me with his arms open. I reached out to hug him.

"You look better," Irene added, approaching me a little more cautiously.

"Yeah, still a bit achy. I will be for a while."

"Hey, guess what?" Vinnie said. He was smiling from ear to ear like a kid on Christmas morning. "I came in first place."

"Congratulations!" I said, giving him a high-five and another hug. "How do you feel now that you're off to the World Series?"

So that was why I didn't see Vinnie at the stadium the previous day; he must have gone into town to celebrate. In all honesty, his flying skills had certainly improved since the first day of the season, and now he'd won the nationals fair and square.

He seemed to be trying hard not to brag about it. "A lot has happened within the last few days and I haven't had a chance to process it all. At the same time, I can't wait to bring it home for America!"

"I actually have something to tell both of you." I hesitated. "I'm leaving the NJRA."

"You've cut your contract?" Irene asked. "What does that mean for you? I take it there must be more to it than just saying goodbye?"

"Once you leave, you're out for good," I said. "I won't even be allowed to talk to either of you anymore."

"But why would you do that?" Vinnie said. "You really want to leave us behind?"

As I kept telling myself, no amount of convincing was going to change what was already done. And it would only be a matter of time before they saw the reality of the NJRA.

"I'm just not happy in the NJRA anymore, and to be fair, I don't think I ever was truly happy about it." I almost mentioned something about the debt, but decided against it. "I don't feel the same way about the whole lifestyle as I did before. There's a darker side to this life of luxury and I've seen enough of it to know that it's not what I want anymore."

I smiled. "But on the bright side, I get to keep a basic pilot's licence, so maybe I'll join a flying club or something just for fun.

I handed the Bruce Dickinson book to Vinnie. "Thought I'd give you this now in case I forget. I can't bring myself to read it anymore, but I know you really enjoyed it."

"Thanks. I'm happy to take it. It's a memento of Max," Vinnie explained. "You might not feel the same way, but I kind of looked up to him ever since I first arrived at Central City."

I didn't know what to say to that.

"You two can help yourself to the rest of my flying books," I huffed.

"You admire Max?" Irene said to Vinnie. "You saw what he did to Jay."

"Guys, let's not talk about this anymore," I changed the subject. "By the way, I'm going to finally get my GED once I leave."

"Sounds like a good plan. Learning is always good," Vinnie said. "I can't wait to start engineering school once the season's over. Then hopefully I can take on a temporary job or two in the off-season."

Five days passed. I began packing all my clothes from the dresser after lunch. Even though I had the rest of the day to pack up, it was better to do it sooner than later. The David Bowie poster had been taken off the wall and placed into my suitcase, along with my medals and trophies from the top of my dresser. At least the NJRA was letting me keep those, though I would probably end up leaving them in a corner of the basement and never looking at them again.

My ears started ringing. To distract myself, I sat down at my computer and opened my music playlist. I deleted the entire folder of Iron Maiden songs, as just the thought of them reminded me of Max and how he'd idolized Bruce Dickinson.

My phone rang. As soon as I saw my adoptive parents' number on the call display, I rejected the call. Then I turned off the phone so they couldn't keep calling me.

My head started to hurt. A nap wasn't a bad idea, especially since I hadn't gotten much sleep the last couple days. I found myself lying in my bed for a good half hour or so, trying to ignore the ringing in my ears and the thoughts of Julianne and Max that wouldn't leave me alone. Finally I fell asleep.

My neck was aching so much that it woke me up from my nap. It was 5:30 p.m. and I'd slept for at least three hours. Julianne and Max's memorial was an hour away.

But what am I going to wear?

I got up and looked at myself in the mirror on my wall. My hair had never been this long before. I pulled the black dress out from my suitcase, knowing I was going to wear it because it would look great on me. I had to make do with what I had, which meant wearing Julianne's dress. The fact that I would be wearing a dead person's clothes to their memorial felt more wrong to me than the fact that the dress was considered women's clothing. But the more I thought about it, the dress felt like a parting gift from Julianne.

It was a knee-length dress on her, but since I was slightly taller than her, it was shorter than that on me. My pilot boots wouldn't go well with the dress, but my dress shoes wouldn't look too bad. A pair of heels or leather platform boots would have been better, but I didn't have any, and Julianne's shoes wouldn't have fit me anyway.

I took out the bottle of phoenix-orange nail polish and

painted my right hand to match my left. It felt a bit awkward to hold the brush in my left hand, since I was right-handed like most of the world. Julianne must have done it enough times that it didn't feel any different to her.

I didn't feel the need to look both ways down the hall when I left my room since I figured the cat was out of the bag already.

Then I heard a gasp from the end of the hallway.

"Good heavens, Julianne, what are you doing here? I must be losing my mind," Mike said.

He took a closer look at me. It felt almost uncomfortable.

"Jay." His tone of voice reminded me of my adoptive mom and his face was turning red. "What's happened to you? Tell me, where'd you get that dress from? That ain't a good look for you."

"I bought it," I stuttered. "At the mall."

Apparently he didn't recognize it from Julianne's wardrobe.

"Julianne's folks are flying in from New York and you're dressed like that?"

"But Vinnie and Irene are okay with it," I responded.

"Why don't you go put on some proper clothes and show some respect?"

There was no point in arguing with him. Soon I would never see him again.

I went back to my room. His definition of proper clothes would be the dress shirt and tie that I hadn't worn in a year. Of course I wanted to show respect, but how was I supposed to respect anyone if they couldn't respect me in return for the way I was? I took the light blue dress shirt out of my suitcase and unfolded it. It could definitely use some ironing.

Should I take off the dress and wear the shirt with my black dress pants? I pondered for a moment, and then changed out of the dress. But these clothes just didn't feel right on me; I felt much better in the dress. I changed back.

My dress shoes didn't look great with it but I had no other shoes to wear.

I tried putting my dress pants on under the dress so they would cover my shoes a bit, as well as my noticeably hairy legs. There was still time to shave my legs, but I didn't want to end up with a bloody mess, since I had never done it before. My dress pants didn't look right under the dress. I remembered that Julianne often wore leggings with her dresses. I went to her room. There was a mumble of voices coming from the lunchroom, meaning that guests were arriving, but the dorm hallway was empty. I looked at the time on my phone; it was 6:00 p.m.; the memorial would start in half an hour.

The first drawer of her dresser was full of various t-shirts and sweaters. The next drawer made a sharp creaking noise as it slid open. I froze like a deer in headlights, even though it was safe to say that there wasn't anyone else around. Next to a couple pairs of designer jeans with sequins and designs stitched on the back pockets, I found a pair of black spandex leggings. I took them out and shut the drawer.

On my way out, I noticed a pair of black leather ankle

boots sitting next to the door. There was not a scuff or scratch on them. They looked slightly bigger and wider than Julianne's other shoes, which could be why they had never been worn. She might have bought them only to realize that they didn't fit her. I picked up the left one and held it next to my foot. I felt like I had struck gold; they were my size.

Back in my room, I shut the door, took off my dress pants and put the black leggings on under the dress. The tight, silky material on my skin sent shivers through my entire body. I took another look at the shirt and pants I had tossed onto the floor. There was no way in hell I was going to wear those instead.

The ankle boots were a bit tight, but I still wanted to wear them. They had a raised heel, about two inches high, which I noticed as I stood up. *So this is what it feels like to wear heels.*

I took a deep breath and opened the door, wiping a few tears from my face. I still felt like I was dragging a huge weight. Everyone at Central City Jet Racing League, including the office staff, would see me at the memorial. I was sweating as I walked down the hallway to the lunchroom, even though I knew that, after the memorial, I wouldn't talk to those people in the room again until who knows when.

Several rows of plastic folding chairs had been set up facing a projector screen at the front. Most of the chairs were taken except for a few. I took a seat next to Vinnie and Irene in the front row on the far right side of the room.

"This seat's taken," Vinnie said.

"Oh, for who?" I replied.

"Wait a second." His jaw dropped as he looked up at my face.

Do I really look that different?

"Jay, you look great," Irene said, smiling. She looked pretty good, too, in her black suit.

"Thanks," I replied. "Mike didn't like it though. He told me to put on some proper clothes, whatever that means. This is certainly proper formal wear."

"Not any more improper than me in a suit," Irene replied.

"It's the first time I've seen you with a suit jacket. It looks great." I said. She blushed.

"As long as it makes you happy," Vinnie said. I could see that he was a little taken aback seeing me in a dress for the first time. "Live life how it lives you."

I was surprised that neither of them seemed to recognize that the dress and leggings I had on had been Julianne's.

Mike walked up to us and pointed at my dress. "What did I say to you earlier?" he scolded.

"Is it really any of your business?" Irene argued.

"I give up," he muttered under his breath. "Just wait until Max's and Julianne's families see you like that."

He went to adjust the projector on the ceiling. A photo slideshow was playing on the screen to soft classical music.

The Erikson family arrived. Izzy was with her mom, Max's ex, as well as two others I assumed were Max's parents and a teenage boy I had never seen before. There was definitely no shortage of height in that family.

The president of the NJRA made his way to the front of the room shortly after the arrival of Julianne's family. The slideshow was paused on two photos of Julianne and Max against a dark blue background as the president gave the introduction.

"Racers, staff, friends, and family, we are gathered here today to celebrate the lives of two very brave and dedicated pilots, Julianne Madison and Kristian Maxwell Erikson, who some of you may know as Max Erikson." His voice was flat and monotonous, like he was reading from a script.

"My name is John Garner, and I'm the president of the National Jet Racing Association. To start off this evening, I'll be bringing up Rita and Amy Madison, Julianne's mother and younger sister, to present the first speeches."

A woman and a teenager walked to the front of the room. John handed the microphone to Julianne's mother.

Rita began speaking, sobbing between her words. "Julianne was such a wonderful daughter. She loved movies and fashion and was the biggest adrenaline junkie in the family. It was only natural for her to be drawn toward jet racing." She paused to take a deep breath. "When she told me that she got accepted to the NJRA's training camp, I was so nervous, but so proud at the same time. When I heard she was going to be flying in the nationals this year, I thought I was dreaming. I could not believe that she was competing in the nationals as a rookie."

Her voice trembled again. "Now, no words can truly describe my heartbreak. When I saw the replay of her slumped over the controls of her plane, I shouted, 'No way, that can't be my Julianne in there!' Life is so fragile."

She passed the microphone to Amy and returned to her seat, blowing her nose with a tissue.

Amy spoke with the same flat tone of voice as John. "Julianne was the best big sister I could ever ask for. I'm really going to miss her love of adventure and trying new things, as well as her great sense of style. I will never forget everything we did like camping, shopping, and that time she made me go on the biggest slide at the water park with her."

She handed the microphone back to John with a blank expression on her face. She looked like she just wanted to go home.

"Thank you, Rita and Amy. My condolences to you. Now, we are going to bring up the members of the Erikson family."

Izzy, her mom, Max's parents, and the teenage boy walked up to the front of the room. The boy looked to be about seventeen. John handed the microphone to Izzy.

"My dad was a great pilot, musician, and, of course a great father. A lot of people talk down about him as being unstable and hotheaded, but if you could see the other side of him, he really was a gentle giant. When I was little, he used to braid my hair and read fairy tales to me whenever he wasn't out playing with his band. In the last five years, he would visit me every weekend after the racing season and we'd go for lunch and movies, and sometimes he would try to teach me how to play the bass. Of course, I'm musically challenged, so I never got too far." Izzy sniffled, but a small smile cracked on her face.

She handed the microphone to Max's father before returning to her seat.

"Mr. Garner, this is a message to you," he began, gritting his teeth. "I don't know what is going on with you and your organization, but this blood sport has got to stop. How could my son have been declared fit to fly after everything he did? I've known Max for the last thirty-five years, and I can assure you this is not his usual behaviour. Do you guys not have some sort of psychological testing for your pilots? What the hell is wrong with your standards? If it weren't for you and your organization, we wouldn't be standing here grieving our hearts out because now we have to bury our eldest son. No parent should ever have to know what this feels like. So you better have a legal team ready, John, because you can bet your ass that you'll be hearing from our family lawyer soon."

He shoved the microphone into John's hand before returning to his seat.

"Thank you, Erikson family," John said in his monotone. "I can only imagine what you are going through. Next, I would like to bring up the program director of Central City Professional Flight Academy, Marianne Lee." John handed the microphone to Marianne.

"It was such a pleasure to have Max spend a day at the academy on behalf of the NJRA. The day began with starstruck students clamouring for autographs and asking questions. Max assisted the flight instructors with a lesson, and the students all went home that day feeling very inspired. Max shared lots of good advice and helped inspire confidence in those who will be doing their first solo flights at the end of the month. All of us at the academy will miss him and the sense of humour and enthusiasm he brought with him during his visit. It is also very heartbreaking for the aviation community to lose such a talented and dedicated pilot."

Marianne walked back to her seat in tears. Irene was next to give her speech.

"I may have only known Julianne for one season, but she was one of the best friends I've ever had in my four years at Central City. She and I were total opposites in many ways, but somehow we managed to put aside our differences and got along so well. She will be greatly missed."

Irene returned to her seat and handed the microphone to Vinnie. He walked to the front of the room.

"It's been an honour knowing Julianne ever since we were in training camp together. While she was quiet and reserved at times, she was such a kind-hearted, hardworking person who loved flying aerobatic. It was always a pleasure flying with her here at Central City Jet Racing League, and I will never forget all those late-night movie and science documentary marathons we used to have." Vinnie started to sob, and then paused to wipe his tears. "I may have only known Max for one season as well, but I learned so much from him about flying, as well as from you, Jay. My first impression of Max when I arrived at Central City was that he was a cocky pilot who was always so full of himself. But after getting to know him, I realized that there was definitely much more to him than that. I'll never forget when he introduced me to Izzy for the first time, because it was only then that I learned that he was such a caring parent who always wanted the best for her. I could only imagine how it feels to not be able to see your own child much for four months straight every year because you're out there racing or preparing for a race."

There he goes, gushing about Max again. What has he become?

"Even though my victory in the nationals was a bit of a fluke, Max was my biggest inspiration ever since I arrived at Central City and flew my first race back in April," Vinnie continued. "I was so impressed by his skills that even though I came in fifteenth place in that race, I was determined to train harder and improve. It was watching Max fly that really made me feel like I was more than just a rookie."

Vinnie handed the microphone back to John and returned to his seat.

What has he become?

CHAPTER 16

My bags had been packed and the closet and dresser had been emptied. The computer was no longer on my desk; it had been packed into a box and loaded onto a folding dolly. The shuttle bus was arriving in half an hour. I was getting ready to leave the Central City Jet Racing League airfield for good; it was a place I would never see again.

I passed by Max and Julianne's dorm rooms on my way out to the league office.

"Need help carrying anything?" Vinnie asked from the end of the hallway. Irene was with him.

I nodded and handed him one of the suitcases.

"Be careful with that," I added. "There're trophies in there."

"What do you plan to do with them?" Irene asked.

"I'm keeping them," I replied. I'd probably just keep them in a box somewhere out of sight so I could take them out and look at them when I felt like remembering my flying days.

"On the subject of trophies, I'm just waiting on mine from the NJRA," Vinnie said. "It'll be here soon. I know it."

THE JET RACER

There was a heavy feeling inside me as I arrived at the front desk of the league office, Vinnie and Irene beside me. It was still hard to believe that this would be the last time I would talk to the two of them. Even if I were to see them at races in the future, I'd be just another nobody in the crowd of thousands.

Al, the office assistant, stood up from behind his desk and came out to greet me.

"Jay, I just need you to sign off on this." He handed me a form. "Could I get your key card as well?"

The form said that I acknowledged that I was no longer with the league. It reminded me of the form I'd signed not long ago to terminate my contract with the NJRA, except this one didn't feel like such a big deal. I picked up the pen and glanced over the form, not that there was very much fine print to it. I already knew there was no turning back for me.

I took the key card out of my pocket and handed it to Al. Then I continued walking toward the door to the parking lot, with Irene and Vinnie by my side. The shuttle bus was waiting for me. Irene leaned over and gave me a hug. "It's been great flying with you the last two years."

"You know, you inspired me so much," I replied, sniffling. "Not only in the sky, but also to discover and accept myself for who I really am, and to be open about it."

"I'm proud of you, Jay," she said. "Just remember, it doesn't matter what you wear or what anyone else says. You're still you and nothing will ever change that."

I gave her one more hug before turning toward Vinnie.

"You wouldn't believe how much I learned from you,"

he said, handing me back my suitcase. He gave me a hug as well. "Even though I've only known you for one season."

I could feel the tears coming as I thought back on all the times we'd spent in his dorm room watching science documentaries, listening to music, and chatting about whatever was on our minds.

"Good luck in Singapore," I replied. "Don't think, just fly."

"Hell, yeah! I'm bringing home the trophy for America!"

Look at him. What is he doing to himself?

As I stepped out into the parking lot, I took one last look at the Central City Jet Racing League airfield. I waved my last goodbye to Irene and Vinnie as they stood in the doorway, then walked over to the shuttle bus. I guessed Mike wasn't going to bother wishing me farewell, but then again, he had probably gone through enough people coming and going over all his years as league caretaker. I wasn't even sure I wanted a farewell from him after all the trouble he had given me about my choice of outfit at the memorial. But like Irene said, it wasn't me that was wrong, but rather those who couldn't accept me as I was.

"We're going to the NJRA apartments, correct?" the driver asked as he helped load everything in. I nodded.

"Actually, could we make a stop for groceries?" I added. I remembered that the only food I had at my apartment was a couple boxes of dry spaghetti.

As we drove along the main street, a large banner in the front window of a restaurant caught my attention. On it were the words "#67 Max Erikson" with "We Will Miss You" below. It was covered with what looked like handwritten messages from fans. There was a similar banner in the window of the sports bar next door, this one with a photo of Max standing next to his plane on it and "67" in black block numbers in the top right-hand corner. Several houses had posters in their window saying "RIP Max Erikson" and "#67 We Love You". There were even a few "Six Foot Six Will Finish Quick" posters from before the nationals that had not been taken down.

I'd been seeing these kinds of posters everywhere for long enough. At this point, I couldn't care any less about them. But I teared up when I saw a single house with "RIP Julianne Madison, Too Beautiful to Die" painted on one of the windows.

What has this all come to? She's dead and all they can talk about are her looks.

It brought back memories of the first day she arrived at Central City Jet Racing League and of showing her how I do my vertical loops. It also brought back memories of her telling me about how she wanted to fly in the West Coast Aerobatics Open in August.

There were plenty more "RIP Max" banners and posters after that. I stared down at my hands to avoid having to look at any more of those posters. The nails on my left hand were still painted phoenix-orange, though some of it was starting to chip off.

"Could you turn the radio up?" I asked the driver, hoping that would distract me from all the Max memorabilia.

"You are listening to *Today Talk* on Central Radio CRC-

FM 101.5. Joining us in the studio today is Don Nunez, vice president of the NJRA. Don, what are your thoughts about the tragic events at the nationals this year?"

"On behalf of the NJRA, I would like to express our deepest sympathies to the Erikson and Madison families in these difficult times. We value the wellbeing of our racers greatly, which is why we take many steps to ensure the safety of our pilots. With that being said, we are banning shoes from future events after pilot Ash Christie almost lost an eye from all the shoes lobbed at him in the chaos following the third round of the nationals."

No shoes allowed? That was completely ridiculous.

"So you're saying that everyone has to walk around barefoot?" the host asked. "I see so many safety issues with that. What if someone stepped on a nail or something?"

"What I'm saying is that attendees will have to leave their shoes in their cars. They will have to wear hotel-style disposable slippers at all of our events. You see, shoes are a dangerous weapon, and we don't allow dangerous weapons in our stadiums. They can easily knock someone out if thrown hard enough, which I have no doubt that someone who's had enough to drink is capable of doing. It's like why drinks are served in plastic cups at most stadiums instead of cans and bottles."

"For sure, I get it," the host replied.

"Shoes can be a hiding place for dangerous items too. Weapons, explosives, I tell you," Don added. "With disposable slippers, there are no hiding places."

He is completely out of his mind. I might not have been a

member of the NJRA anymore, but I had a feeling this shoe policy wouldn't get very far.

"Thank you for your time, Don. I'm sending my condolences to the Madison and Erikson families as well."

The bus stopped in front of Roy's Grocery, a small local store. I'd never been there before, as I usually went to bigger chain stores because they were cheaper.

"Here you go," the driver said as he parked the bus. "I'll wait for you out here."

I never paid much attention to the newspapers and magazines in the lineup while waiting to pay for groceries, but the front cover of a gossip magazine caught my eye: "Max Erikson's black box recovered: Findings from the flight data recorder." In smaller text below it was "Shocking results of Julianne Madison's autopsy LEAKED: Two months pregnant at time of death?"

Julianne? Pregnant? My jaw dropped. I would never have guessed, but then again, two months was pretty early. *Why would she keep it a secret from everyone?* It was more likely she hadn't even known herself, as the NJRA wouldn't have allowed her to continue flying if she had reported that she was pregnant.

I grabbed the magazine from the rack and placed it onto the counter next to my groceries. There was another magazine next to it on the rack, but I left it alone, even though its frontpage headline caught my eye: "Unusual eating habits, mood swings, talk of suicide, and other unusual activity during the weeks leading to up this year's nationals."

The cashier looked almost surprised as he rang up the

magazine. Maybe it was because so few people actually bought magazines anymore. Most people just skimmed through them while waiting in line.

"That'll be $62.70," the cashier said.

I returned to the shuttle bus with my groceries and the magazine, which I could not wait to read. We passed many more Max-related messages on posters and window art. There wasn't anything for Julianne after the window art on that house I'd seen earlier. Most of the population of Central City had been fans of Max ever since his first win at the nationals four years before.

We pulled up at the NJRA apartments. "Be careful with that," I said to the driver as he unloaded the box with my computer in it. He placed my two suitcases on the ground.

I struggled to pick up the two full bags of groceries from under the seat. They felt as though they were full of cinderblocks.

"Do you need a hand with that?" the driver asked.

I nodded, huffing as I suddenly got emotional again. He unfolded the dolly and placed my computer box on it, and the two bags of groceries on top of that. I took one of my suitcases from him.

"Which floor are you on?"

"Second floor, apartment 203."

I tapped my key fob on the scanner at the front door. He followed me into the elevator with the dolly and my other suitcase. It felt odd to be returning to the NJRA apartments before the end of the season.

The elevator stopped at the second floor.

"It's just around the corner, not far," I said. The driver helped carry my belongings into the apartment.

"Well, Jay, I wish you the best in whatever's to come," the driver said in an emotionless voice, with a smile that seemed forced.

I needed to start looking for a place to stay since they would be kicking me out in a month's time. I put the groceries onto the dining table and pulled the magazine out of the bag before throwing it onto the couch to read later. Then I unpacked my computer from the box.

I unzipped one of my suitcases. My NJRA hoodie was at the top of everything.

"Fly, Jay, fly," I said as I tossed the hoodie into the corner of the room.

I didn't even feel like reading the magazine anymore. I noticed how quiet it was in the apartment. They must have replaced the air conditioning units while I wasn't there. I turned on the TV, hoping that a bit of background noise would help block out that high-pitched ringing in my ears.

"Tonight at six, join us for an exclusive inside look at the events of the NJRA Nationals, featuring the views of two leading aviation safety consultants."

That caught my attention just as I was about to pick up the phone to call my adoptive parents. I looked up at the TV. Slow-motion footage of Max crashing into the mountain was being shown, followed by another video of the moment when Max sheared off a good portion of my wing.

I felt as though everything had come to a standstill, like I was frozen in time. I didn't even try to hold back the tears. I

ANDY DAVIDS

missed them, Max and Julianne. And I missed Vinnie and Irene too, knowing that I'd never be able to talk to them again. I allowed myself to let it all out, to grieve, to feel what it all felt like, once and for all. The echoes inside my head of my classmates giving me the whole boys-don't-cry deal the first time I fell off the monkey bars on the playground didn't matter anymore. I had never known before what it felt like to really lose a friend or rather, a few. It wasn't just in terms of death. I was all alone now, with nobody by my side who understood me.

I pulled Julianne's floral blouse out of my suitcase. It was all wrinkled and smelled of sweat, but I put it on anyway. I planned to wash it with the rest of my laundry. The familiar comfort of wearing it came back to me. I'd probably wear it again when the time felt right.

After several minutes, I was ready to call my adoptive parents to let them know what was going on. My adoptive mom picked up the phone.

"I quit the NJRA." I could feel a lump in my throat as I said it. I almost wanted to make up an entire story about how I was going to work in the pits instead.

"Why? I thought you love being in the NJRA."

"I cut my contract."

"How come?"

"I'm not allowed to fly anymore. I literally don't see any reason for staying."

"That's your choice. You have a lot to take care of, so just take things one step at a time for now."

"Right now, I need to find a place to live. I have to

leave here in a month," I explained.

"Then you should focus on that first and worry about the rest when the time comes. You've got time to look around. Besides, if you don't find anything, you can always stay with us."

I didn't even want to think about that option.

"Something's burning on the stove, I have to go now." I hung up.

I flipped through the TV channels to see if there was anything worth watching. On the way to the hard rock music channel, a news channel caught my attention.

"A week after the devastating events at the NJRA Nationals, investigations continue into the deaths of Julianne Madison and Max Erikson. Jet racer Andrew Mayer has been suspended from the NJRA following accusations of foul play. On the phone with us live from Boston, Massachusetts, is Kelly Mayer, mother of Andrew Mayer, with her side of the story."

A picture of her appeared on the screen with her name above it.

"Mrs. Mayer, following the back-to-back tragedies and your son's suspension from the NJRA, investigators are naming him as a potential suspect. You've mentioned that he should not be getting this kind of press," the news anchor said.

"As the son of a retired NJRA pilot, Andrew has always had a passion for aviation," she said. "And just like my husband, he's probably the most easygoing person I've ever known. He's also the most hardworking person in our whole family. He made the honour roll every year of high school and was even offered a scholarship to the University of Massachusetts, which he turned down to pursue NJRA training camp."

I rolled my eyes. Andrew got a suspension from the NJRA and then his mom went to the news to blabber on and on about how he must have been innocent because he was an honour roll student. So if I had stayed in school and got straight A's and scholarships, would someone have come to my defense even if I'd sabotaged a plane?

"I see," said the anchor. "Would you like to elaborate on the accusations?"

"When I first heard about the accusations, I said to my husband, 'No way, that's just not him,'" Kelly replied. "I mean, sure, he can be a bit emotional sometimes, as most of us can be, but he wouldn't do something that extreme over… what? An engine failure?"

"So you are saying that the anger and negativity that's been directed toward your son is uncalled for?" the news anchor said.

"Well, it's not just about him anymore. We've been getting a whole lot of hateful emails, ranging from accusations that we're bad parents to threats to set our house on fire. There've even been death threats against our family."

"I heard that your home was vandalized as well. Can you confirm that?"

"Last night we had rocks thrown at our front windows. The alarm was going off and the dog was barking; the whole nine yards. When I looked out the window, I saw someone had thrown a pile of dirty diapers and used cat litter all over our lawn and covered our hedge with fish guts. My husband and I have been up since three this morning and I was so afraid to go out that I had to ask our neighbour to walk the dog."

A photo of the front of the house was shown on the screen. The windows were broken, the walls were covered with graffiti of stick people performing sexual acts, and the front yard was littered with dirty diapers.

I turned off the TV. Andrew's mom's voice was getting unbearable.

My mind jumped around, from Vinnie and Irene to apartment searching and then back to Vinnie and Irene. It had only been a few hours ago that I'd said my last goodbyes to them. I felt really tired. *I need a nap.*

I lay down on the couch, but my mind kept racing. It was Andrew's mom's voice, what I heard of it in those few minutes before I shut off the TV. I wasn't sure who I was angrier at; Andrew, as it was most likely that he'd been responsible, or his mom for trying to defend him. I could not help but feel that his family deserved what had been done to their house.

Eventually, I was so exhausted that I passed right out.

It was 6:02 p.m. when I woke up. I sat up on the couch and turned on the TV, crossing my fingers that Andrew's mom wouldn't show up again.

Photos of Max taken throughout the years and various video clips from races he'd flown in were shown as a voice said, "After a bloody end to this year's NJRA Nationals that resulted in the deaths of racers Max Erikson and Julianne Madison, the investigations continue. Tonight, Chris Land brings you an exclusive inside look featuring the views of experts in aviation safety, who are saying that Erikson should never have been allowed to fly in the nationals due to obvious signs of emotional instability on the day preceding the crash."

The camera switched to the TV studio.

"My name is Chris Land and you are watching *Current Perspectives*. We begin by bringing you the initial findings from the analysis of Max Erikson's black box, which was recently recovered from the wreckage near West Coast Airsports Stadium in Utah County. With us in the studio today are aviation safety experts Carl Dietrich and Eliza Jacobsen, who have both reviewed the black box recording."

The two experts were shown sitting behind a desk like the ones news reporters usually have.

Chris Land continued. "In the recording we are about to play, there is no radio communication heard, indicating that Erikson's radio was switched off. What you are about to hear are Erikson's final words right before the crash."

The voice on the recording was pretty muffled, but it was clearly Max's. I couldn't make out what he was saying through most of the recording, though I definitely heard my name in there.

"It sounds pretty clearly like, 'Fly, Jay, fly,'" Carl Dietrich said.

I felt a shiver in my spine. They played the recording again. It definitely sounded like "Fly, Jay, fly."

"There is no doubt that is Max Erikson's voice on the

recording," Eliza added. "But you have to remember, we tend to hear what we want to hear when it's not clear. It's a way our brains trick us. We often jump to conclusions based on what we think we perceive, but the reality could be something completely different. It's like when you've been listening to a song for so long that you're pretty sure you know all the words to it, but then when you look up the lyrics, they're completely different."

"It would make sense that he said something like that," Carl replied. "The fact that his radio as well as his transponder had been intentionally shut off at the time of the crash leads me to believe that he had a sinister intention. Under normal circumstances, the only reason a pilot would ever shut down their transponder is if the system had malfunctioned or short circuited. Black box data reveals that Erikson's transponder was switched off about two minutes prior to the crash, with no evidence of malfunction."

Why would Max have flown off course deliberately? It seemed like he was trying to lure me off course so he could crash into me. All he was afraid of was that I would out-compete him for Julianne's love just like he would out-compete me in the races, when I wanted no part of his perverted fantasies. I'd thought all he wanted was to win the nationals again.

"The fact that the NJRA has only released five seconds of the cockpit recording leads me to believe that there was more to it that they're holding back," Eliza said. "You have to remember, a big corporation like the NJRA wants to protect its own reputation."

ANDY DAVIDS

A photo of Julianne standing next to her plane at the Nationals was shown. I could feel my eyes tearing up and my hands getting sweaty.

"Thank you, Carl and Eliza. We will now have someone from the NJRA's Health and Safety Committee join us on the phone from the NJRA head office," Chris said.

The screen cut to a photo of Lee McLean from the NJRA's Health and Safety Committee. I recognized him as one of the two who had asked me a bunch of questions after round two of the nationals.

"Thanks, Chris," Lee said on the phone.

"From the beginning of the NJRA season, Erikson allegedly expressed affection toward rookie Julianne Madison at times," Chris began. "Erikson stated in interviews that he'd been single ever since his divorce with ex-wife, Francine Ryan, though it is well known that he enjoyed the company of women. Is it possible that Madison's death had pushed him over the edge?"

I was surprised he didn't mention that Julianne had been pregnant. A video clip of Max grabbing my arms and pinning me against the hangar wall came up on the screen. Sitting on the couch, I swore I could smell WD-40.

"The most prominent display of emotional instability came after round two of the nationals, when Erikson was involved in a fight with fellow racer Jay Smith before being removed from the area by stadium security," Lee explained following the clip.

I cringed as soon as I heard my name in that sentence.

"Thanks, Lee," Chris said.

The screen then cut to a photo of Dr. Allen.

"Dr. Christopher Allen, medical examiner for the NJRA, performed assessments on all of the pilots attending the nationals, in accordance with the association's guidelines. NJRA protocols require all pilots involved in an event where there has been a serious injury or death to undergo psychological assessment before being allowed to continue flying. Dr. Allen is currently undergoing questioning from investigators. He has declined an interview with us. After the break, we will have an exclusive interview with Francine Ryan, Erikson's ex-wife, as well as with Erikson's daughter, Izzy Erikson."

A commercial for the live broadcast of the West Coast Aerobatics Open came on. It showed video clips from the previous year's competition set to hard rock music. It was difficult to think that it was only a month away and I wasn't going to be in it. I reached for the TV remote, wanting to shut off the ad. But I hesitated, and then put it back down. I really wanted to watch the rest of the *Current Perspectives* special. The commercial break ended. Francine Ryan came up on the screen.

"Francine, what are your thoughts on the whole situation?" the interviewer asked.

"I just don't get why Max should have been flying at all, especially in a sport where such aggressive and even violent competition is expected," Francine replied. "I mean, Max was no stranger to the world of anger issues; it's what destroyed our marriage so many years ago."

A photo of the Silver Room nightclub was shown on

the screen.

"The singer of a band that played at the Silver Room nightclub three years ago testified in court that he received bruises and broken fingers during an altercation with Erikson," Chris explained. "The singer, Robert Stevens, testified that Erikson kicked over a microphone stand a couple minutes into the first song of the set, damaging a wireless microphone. Stevens testified that he immediately recognized Erikson, having shared the stage with him years before and claimed that Erikson came into the Silver Room looking for trouble. Stevens gave Erikson the middle finger. Stevens testified that Erikson became infuriated and accused him of sleeping with Erikson's girlfriend at the time, Lana Clayton. Erikson then dragged him by the shirt collar and slammed him against a speaker cabinet at the back of the stage."

A security camera recording of the scene was shown with the video pausing and zooming in at certain parts.

"Erikson pleaded guilty to charges of assault, which were later dropped. Erikson was dropped by a few of his sponsors once the charges went public, but was nonetheless allowed to fly in the following NJRA seasons without restriction."

The screen cut back to the interview with Francine Ryan.

"Sixteen years ago, I married my best friend. Seven years ago, he burned our house to the ground. And for all those years between, every time he got mad, he blamed it on me. This was no way to be a role model for Izzy."

I turned off the TV. I felt like I'd had enough, even if it

meant missing the interview with Izzy. Besides, I was sure there would be plenty more Max news over the coming days.

I was surprised how well I'd been able to hold back the tears, but after turning off the TV I found myself immediately reaching for the tissue box. After a good cry, I decided to put on Julianne's black dress and leggings that I had worn to the memorial. As I looked at myself in the mirror, I felt a bit better until the memories of the first day of the season, when Julianne first arrived at Central City Jet Racing League, hit me again.

Pulling myself together, I decided that I might as well get a start on that pile of laundry. I picked up the NJRA hoodie that I had tossed aside and threw it into the basket with everything else. I brought the basket to the laundry room. I had no second thoughts about going down the hallway dressed as I was, even though nobody else was around, other than maybe the building custodian.

As I loaded the washer, the memories of Julianne were quickly pushed aside by a memory from not too long back. It was a memory of that time when Vinnie and I stayed up listening to music during the thunderstorm and he told me his story of the giggling motion-activated baby doll. Except now it felt like the thunderstorm was inside me, and the giggling baby doll was the echo of Julianne's voice in the back of my head, asking me for tips on aerobatic manoeuvres.

ANDY DAVIDS

Creative writing has long been part of Andy Davids's life, having started with writing fanfiction at a young age and later progressing to poetry and short stories. While attending Selkirk College in 2016, Davids completed their first full-length novel, The Jet Racer.

Some of their favourite authors include Stephen King, Scott Westerfeld, Haruki Murakami, David L. Robbins, and Isaac Asimov. Aside from being an author, Davids has also been an audio engineer, a music teacher, a babysitter, and an office assistant. When not writing, Davids can be found caring for their goldfish aquarium, serving meals to people in need in their community, watching documentary films, playing board games, using synthesizers to create electronic music, and reading up on random facts that may or may not be included in future works.